MONTANA
Mavericks:
Return to Whitehorn—

*Welcome to Whitehorn, Montana—
the home of bold men and daring women.
A place where rich tales of passion
and adventure are unfolding under the Big Sky.
Seems this charming little town has some mighty
big secrets. And everybody's talking about...*

Dana Bailey—She's a city slicker on the run—but nobody knows it. And now that she's witnessed a holdup in rustic Whitehorn, it looks as if she'll be around for a while. Maybe even long enough for someone to discover her secret....

Kurt Noble—Whitehorn's sexiest lawman seems to have taken a fancy to the town newcomer. But he can also sense when someone is lying to him. He and Miss Dana are the hot topic at the Hip Hop Café, and some folks are sayin' that the secretive señorita may just prove to be Kurt's downfall....

J.D. Cade—The town's mystery man just happened to be on hand to foil that holdup. Funny how he keeps showing up all over the place! Could he have some connection to Dana? Or does he have some deeper tie to Whitehorn's affairs?

Dear Reader,

Spring is in the air! It's the perfect time to pick wildflowers, frolic outdoors…and fall in love. And this March, Special Edition has an array of love stories that set the stage for romance!

Bestselling author Victoria Pade delivers an extra-special THAT SPECIAL WOMAN! title. The latest installment in her popular A RANCHING FAMILY series, *Cowboy's Love* is about a heroine who passionately reunites with the rugged rancher she left behind. Don't miss this warm and wonderful tale about love lost—and found again.

Romantic adventure is back in full force this month when the MONTANA MAVERICKS: RETURN TO WHITEHORN series continues with *Wife Most Wanted* by Joan Elliott Pickart—a spirited saga about a wanted woman who unwittingly falls for the town's sexiest lawman! And don't miss *Marriage by Necessity,* the second book in Christine Rimmer's engaging CONVENIENTLY YOURS miniseries.

Helen R. Myers brings us *Beloved Mercenary,* a poignant story about a gruff, brooding hero who finds new purpose when a precious little girl—and her beautiful mother—transform his life. And a jaded businessman gets much more than he bargained for when he conveniently marries his devoted assistant in *Texan's Bride* by Gail Link. Finally this month, to set an example for his shy teenage son, a confirmed loner enters into a "safe" relationship with a pretty stranger in *The Rancher Meets His Match* by Patricia McLinn.

I hope you enjoy this book, and each and every story to come!

Sincerely,

Tara Gavin
Senior Editor and Editorial Coordinator

Please address questions and book requests to:
Silhouette Reader Service
U.S.: 3010 Walden Ave., P.O. Box 1325, Buffalo, NY 14269
Canadian: P.O. Box 609, Fort Erie, Ont. L2A 5X3

JOAN ELLIOTT PICKART

WIFE MOST WANTED

SPECIAL EDITION®

Published by Silhouette Books
America's Publisher of Contemporary Romance

Special thanks and acknowledgment are given to
Joan Elliott Pickart for her contribution to the
Montana Mavericks: Return to Whitehorn series.

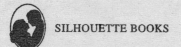 SILHOUETTE BOOKS

ISBN 0-373-24160-7

WIFE MOST WANTED

JOAN ELLIOTT PICKART

is the author of over seventy novels. When she isn't writing, she enjoys watching football, knitting, reading, gardening and attending craft shows on the town square. Joan has three all-grown-up daughters and a fantastic little grandson. In September of 1995 Joan traveled to China to adopt her fourth daughter, Autumn. Joan and Autumn have settled into their cozy cottage in a charming small town in the high pine country of Arizona.

WANTED

Have you seen this woman?
Dana Bailey, 28 years old
5' 8", Blond hair, Blue eyes
Wanted for questioning
in Chicago felony case
Last seen in the company
of a certain lawman
in Whitehorn, Montana

WARNING:

Suspect may be dangerous—
to the lawman's heart

Chapter One

Dana Bailey rotated her neck back and forth as she drove, then frowned as she glanced quickly at her watch.

It was only a little after five o'clock in the morning, she thought, and she was already tired, felt as though the day should be half over. Well, in a way it was, as she'd been driving since around 3:00 a.m.

She'd been unable to sleep much...again. She'd tossed and turned, then been plagued by nightmares when she managed to doze.

The problem was, she thought dismally, even when she was awake she was in the midst of the real nightmare her life had become.

It was all so unbelievable, but horrifyingly true. In just two weeks she'd gone from being a respected and successful attorney in Chicago to a fugitive on the run from the authorities. Dear God, it was so frightening, so...

"Stop it," she said aloud.

There was no time to feel sorry for herself. She knew, just knew, that if she ever started crying over the living nightmare she was now existing in, ever released her tight hold on her emotions, she'd collapse, just dissolve into a weeping mess and give up.

"No," she said, smacking the steering wheel of her compact car with one hand.

She was going to prove that she was innocent...somehow. In the meantime, she was continually on the move, keeping off the main turnpikes and freeways and staying in small towns at night.

Where was she now? she wondered, looking down quickly at the map next to her on the seat. Yes, all right. She was about a two-hour drive from Whitehorn, Montana. Whitehorn, Blackhorn, what difference did it make? As long as it was tucked out of the way and she did nothing to draw attention to herself it suited her purposes just fine.

She needed a few things from a store, so in a couple of hours she'd go shopping in Whitehorn, Montana.

"Hooray," she said dryly.

They were out there again.

Kurt Noble groaned in frustration, then rolled onto his back on the bed. He took the pillow with him, covering his head and pressing fists into the pillow where it fell over his ears.

It was no use. He could still hear them, and he would have sworn that every one wore a Rolex watch that informed them when it was 5:00 a.m.

When he'd arrived back in Whitehorn three weeks ago to take up temporary residency in his deceased mother's house, they hadn't been there on the first day.

Then, he was convinced, the word had gone out, through some strange means of communication.

The very next morning there had been two, announcing their presence at 5:00 a.m. Now, three weeks later, the count was up to at least a dozen and, damn it, they were loud.

And right on time. Five a.m.

Mumbling an earthy expletive, Kurt threw the pillow aside, followed by the blankets, then he left the bed. He snatched up sweat pants from the floor, pulled them on, then strode from the bedroom, a glower on his beard-roughened face.

Sunlight flooded the small living room, the cheery glow promising a cool, Montana-perfect spring day in May. At the moment, Kurt didn't give a rip what the weather offered.

He entered the kitchen, grabbed a huge bag leaning against a cupboard, retraced his steps, then went straight to the front door, flinging it open.

"I hear you. Okay?" he said gruffly. "So shut the hell up. Okay? Oh, man, I don't need this."

Shoving open the creaking screen door, he stepped out onto the sagging wood front porch, his appearance increasing the volume of noise from the assembled group. He did a quick count of the unwelcome visitors.

"Thirteen," he said aloud. "Dandy, just great. That's a nice, crummy, unlucky number. Hey! You guys are driving me nuts. Read my lips. *I don't like cats.*"

The thirteen felines were not put off in the least by their host's grumpy mood. They meowed and yowled as they wove around Kurt's feet and ankles.

"All right, all right, move," he said, managing to inch forward.

Kurt poured dry food into the row of bowls on the porch, the same bowls that had been there for as long as he could remember. A baby bathtub filled with water was at the far end of the line.

The cats dashed for their breakfast and began to eat. Blessed silence fell.

Kurt stood quietly and watched the hungry crew devouring the meal. He glanced heavenward.

"Are you watching this, Mom?" he said, his voice gentling. "I'm doing this for you, you know. You spoiled all these stray yo-yos for years, and now I'm stuck with them."

A breeze whispered across the porch, and Kurt smiled in spite of himself. He turned and went back into the house, making certain none of the pesty cats managed to follow him inside.

He drew the line at letting any of them in the house, he thought, heading for the kitchen again. His mother might not have been able to resist the beasts' pleas to come in, but he sure could.

One of the memories of his youth was the necessity to remove a furry bundle from wherever he wished to sit. Cats. There had always been a zillion cats inside and outside the Noble home.

In the kitchen, Kurt plunked the bag against the counter, then began to prepare a pot of coffee, yawning several times in the process.

Yes, cats, he thought. They were just one of the unpleasant things he remembered about growing up in this small, weather-beaten structure. But he had no intention of dragging out the remaining memories.

With a mug of steaming, strong coffee finally in hand, Kurt sank onto a metal chair at the chipped Formica table at the end of the room. He took a sip, nodded in satisfaction, then stared moodily into space.

Full circle, he thought suddenly. He'd sat at this table when he was so little his feet stuck straight out in front of him and his chin nearly rested on his plate.

Now he was thirty-five years old, and the feet on his six-foot frame definitely reached the floor.

He was back in Whitehorn, Montana, where he'd been born and raised. Full circle.

But he wasn't a boy anymore, a child who believed in Santa Claus and the tooth fairy and dreams of what the future had yet to bring. There was a sprinkle of gray in his thick, short dark hair, and the lines of a life that had not been gentle were etched on his face.

And just inches above his heart was an angry red puckered scar, created when a bullet had torn through him, nearly costing him his life.

Kurt took a deep swallow of coffee.

The discoloration of the wound would fade some in time, he supposed, as would the hot pain that still rocketed throughout him when he strained the damaged area. The healing wasn't quite complete, not yet.

But the memories of how and why he'd been shot? The emotional pain he'd suffered along with the physical? The lesson he'd learned about trusting and loving the wrong person...again? None of those would dim in his mind or his heart. Not ever. And they shouldn't. They were his just deserts for being a damn fool...in spades.

Kurt drained the mug, then got to his feet. He deposited the mug in the sink, then hesitated, realizing the sink was so full of dirty dishes that the balancing mug on top might cause an avalanche.

Tonight, he thought, thudding the mug onto the counter, he'd wash the dishes. Now *there* was an exciting event to look forward to all day.

Chuckling at the extent of his own rotten mood, Kurt left the kitchen, his destination the bathroom, for a shave and a hot shower.

While he stood under the shower's rejuvenating hot spray, the term *full circle* echoed in Kurt's mind again.

That he was back in Whitehorn, albeit temporarily, was as much of a surprise to him as it was to some of the people in town.

He'd just received clearance from the doctor to return to work on the Seattle police force on a restricted basis, which was a fancy way of saying he was to keep his butt on a chair behind a desk. For an undercover cop, the prospect of being cooped up in an office all day held no appeal whatsoever.

But there had been more than just the dislike of the offered desk job bothering him, Kurt knew. During the long weeks of recuperation, which included physical therapy, a seed of restlessness within him had been nurtured by the idle hours.

He'd finally admitted to himself that the idea of returning to work on the force in any capacity didn't evoke one iota of enthusiasm.

The whole episode leading up to his being shot had cost him, physically *and* mentally. He was a burned-out cop, a bruised and battered man, pure and simple.

He needed... Hell, there had been the rub. He

hadn't known *what* he needed, but the answer sure as hell hadn't been in Seattle.

Then he'd received a telephone call from his sister, Leigh, who lived in Whitehorn with her husband and two kids. He and Leigh had always been close, had leaned on each other during their traumatic childhood.

Leigh had been terrified when Kurt was shot, had not breathed a sigh of relief until she heard him tell her on the phone that he was just too plain ornery to die.

But it had been the last call from Leigh that took him out of Seattle on an official leave of absence.

Detective Dakota Winston Calloway, Leigh had told Kurt, was expecting her second child, and had just put in for maternity leave from the Blue Lake County Sheriff's Department. Sheriff Judd Hensley was now short one detective on the force.

"You could contact Judd," Leigh had said. "It seems to me that full-time work here in laid-back Whitehorn would be equal to the restricted basis you're looking at there in Seattle. Don't you think so?"

Kurt had chuckled. "You're probably right. Whitehorn isn't exactly the high-crime capital of the country." He paused. "Although the old hometown has had an amazing amount of trouble in the past."

"That's the truth," Leigh had said, sighing. "There was the murder of that Floyd Oakley at Dugin and Mary Jo Kincaid's wedding, then Dugin himself was murdered later. The finding of Charles Avery's body after all those years was big news, too."

"Leigh…"

"Then, oh, mercy, the kidnapping of baby Jennifer," Leigh had gone on. "The whole town was so upset then. It was awful. I can remember having trouble sleeping during the weeks that Jennifer was missing. I kept getting up in the night to check on Max and Chloe. I had to continually reassure myself that my children were tucked safely in their beds.

"My heart ached so much for Sterling and Jessica McCallum while they waited for news about their little girl. Jennifer is their adopted daughter, but they love her every bit as much as I love my two children. What a party Whitehorn put on when baby Jennifer was found alive and well."

"Leigh…"

"I'm sorry. I'm babbling, and you hate it when I talk your leg off. Anyway, Kurt, all those gruesome things were cleared up in one swoop when it was revealed that Mary Jo Kincaid was actually Lexine Baxter. She grew up in Whitehorn, you know. But nobody recognized her after all these years because she'd had plastic surgery. Mary Jo, Lexine, whatever you want to call her, was arrested for the whole kit and caboodle, including the murders of Jeremiah Kincaid and baby Jennifer's birth mother."

"Yeah, she was one busy lady," Kurt had said.

"She was a horrible, evil woman, with no hint of being a lady."

"Your point, chatter cheeks?"

"My point, little brother, is that Whitehorn is back to normal. Dakota told me that no one on the force has put in overtime in ages. It's business as usual. Oh, Kurt, please call Judd Hensley. I just know he'd be thrilled to have you fill in for Dakota. You're so bummed about staring desk duty in the face there in Seattle, and this is the perfect solution.

"You could stay in Mama's house. It might fall

down around your ears, but... Will you think about it?''

''Yeah, I'll think about it, Leigh. I appreciate your call.''

''I love you, Kurt. It would be wonderful to have you back in Whitehorn.''

''It would be a temporary assignment.''

''I realize that, but you'd at least be here for a while. You'll contact Judd?''

''I said I'd *think* about contacting Judd.''

Kurt turned off the water and stepped out of the old claw-foot tub. After drying with a rather thread-bare towel, he walked naked down the hall to his bedroom.

So, he'd called Judd Hensley, he thought, his mind wandering on, and here he was back in Whitehorn for a spell. Full circle. He was putting in his time, allowing his body to heal, and hoping his mind would do the same.

He was also attempting to square off against the fact that the sense of something being missing from his life was still gnawing away at him. It was a question without an answer. A piece absent from the confusing puzzle that was himself.

''Forget it,'' Kurt mumbled as he dressed.

He'd done so much heavy-duty thinking over the past weeks, it was a wonder his brain hadn't blown a circuit. Enough, already.

Clad in gray slacks, a pale blue dress shirt and a darker gray sport coat, Kurt stuffed his tie in his pocket, having no intention of allowing it to strangle him for one second longer than necessary. He'd put it on when he got to the office, just as he'd done each day since becoming a member of Judd's crew, two and a half weeks ago. His gun and handcuffs were clipped to the back of his belt.

Kurt left the house by the back door, having no desire to step over and around the cats on the front porch, who would now be snoozing in the morning sun.

The air was crisp and clear, with not one hint of pollution marring it. The sky was a brilliant blue, dotted with puffs of fluffy clouds.

Kurt drove the fifteen miles into town by rote, every inch of the stretch of road etched indelibly in his mind. He handled the four-wheel-drive vehicle with ease, knowing exactly how the well-maintained vehicle would react to whatever he required it to do.

Twenty minutes later, he parked in front of the Hip Hop Café, which was owned by Melissa Avery North.

Kurt had fallen into the routine of having a hearty breakfast at the café each morning. Lunch depended on where he was and what he was doing. Dinner was his own inept attempt at cooking, which resulted in a periodic sinkful of dishes that he ignored until the last possible moment.

Kurt entered the café, which was bright, welcoming, and beckoning with delicious aromas.

Melissa had decorated the café in a motif that was uniquely her own. The chrome counter and several leather-seated booths hinted of the fifties. The tables and chairs were a mishmash of styles and bright colors; nothing matched but the whole effect somehow worked well.

Large pots of ivy and ferns hung from the ceiling, and an authentic old-fashioned jukebox stood in a place of honor against one wall.

Kurt greeted several people who bid him good-morning, people he'd known all of his life. He slid into one of the booths, not bothering to pick up the menu. A waitress appeared almost immediately at his side and filled his coffee cup.

"Morning, Kurt," the waitress said. "You want the usual?"

"That'll do it, Janie. Thanks."

"You bet."

Kurt watched Janie hurry away, reaffirming in his mind that she was an excellent waitress.

She was very pretty, too, he mused, in a fresh, wholesome sort of way. She wore her long blond hair in a ponytail while working, had expressive blue eyes and a slim figure.

According to Melissa, Janie hadn't been at the Hip Hop very long. She had been attempting to work and attend college to obtain a teaching degree. Exhausted after two years of the grueling pace, she'd quit school to work full-time and save her money. She was twenty-four years old, and her dream of being a teacher was on hold, not forgotten or abandoned.

Kurt nodded slightly.

He hoped Janie's goal became a reality for her, he thought. He admired and respected her tenacity and drive. And he envied her ability to still dream.

Yes, Janie was a top-notch waitress. Well, she was unless that guy...what was his name?...he used initials. Yeah, J. D. Cade...came into the café.

Kurt chuckled softly.

He'd been there one morning when J. D. Cade had come in, slid onto a stool at the counter and ordered a cup of coffee. Janie had lost it. The guy was only a wrangler at the Kincaid ranch, but the way Janie acted, you'd have thought he was a movie star. No one watching her would ever have known that she was an efficient better-than-most waitress.

That Janie Carson had a crush on J. D. Cade had been no newsflash, after what Kurt witnessed that morning. She'd filled J.D.'s coffee cup until it overflowed into the saucer, then followed that by knocking his water glass into his lap.

Kurt had to give J. D. Cade, whoever he was, credit for the way he'd handled the situation, though. Janie had obviously been about to burst into embarrassed tears, but J.D. had waved off the cold dunking, saying a little water never hurt a pair of dusty ranch jeans.

"Enjoy," Janie said, placing a platter-size plate in front of Kurt and bringing him out of his thoughts. "The usual, sir…pancakes, two eggs over easy, hash browns, bacon and toast." She topped off his coffee cup.

"Should hold me till lunch," Kurt said, picking up his fork.

Janie laughed, then moved on to the next booth.

Kurt devoted his full attention to his enormous breakfast.

Dana drove slowly along the main street of Whitehorn, being extremely careful to stay well within the speed limit. The last thing in the world she needed was to be stopped by a police officer for speeding. The image in her mind of that scenario was chilling.

She spotted a convenience store with an Open sign on the door and parked in front.

A larger grocery store would be less expensive, Dana mused, but she'd already discovered that businesses in small towns hadn't gotten with the program of opening early to accommodate people on the way to work.

She got out of the car, locked it, then stretched, stifling a yawn. As she walked slowly toward the curb, her glance fell on her Illinois license plate.

She was lousy at being a fugitive, she thought. She had bolted in her own car, was using her own name and credit cards, was probably leaving a trail as bright as a neon sign.

But there hadn't been time to think things through, to plan. She'd thrown clothes into suitcases, grabbed her purse and run.

As the days passed, she'd been afraid to stop and rent a car, for fear that the rental agencies had been alerted to be on the watch for her. Besides, she would have had to use her own credit card to rent the vehicle.

Yes, indeed, she was a crummy criminal, she thought, attempting to lighten her bleak frame of mind. She needed a training course in being on the lam from the law.

Dana rolled her eyes heavenward at her own dark humor, then quickened her step and entered the store. Nodding politely at the elderly gentleman behind the counter, she lifted a small plastic basket from the stack by the door and made her way down the first aisle.

She dropped a bottle of shampoo into the basket, having found out that the small, off-the-beaten-track motels she stayed in did not offer amenities like pretty sample-size shampoos and lotions.

A package of disposable razors followed the shampoo, then a jar of moisturizing cream. Her attention was caught by a selection of magazines and books, and she treated herself to a copy of a bestseller now out in paperback.

Maybe, just maybe, she thought, she could escape from her own real-life drama for a few hours by reading someone else's fictitious one.

About to start toward the checkout counter, Dana decided a cold soda with plenty of sugar and caffeine was just what she needed to sip on as she drove out of Whitehorn.

She retraced her steps to the back wall, removed a can of soda from the refrigerated section, then walked quickly in the direction of the checkout, the soda can still in her hand.

"Nobody move!" a male voice shouted.

Dana halted dead in her tracks, her eyes widening with horror when she saw a man pointing a gun at the elderly gentleman behind the counter.

"Stay right there, lady," the man with the gun said to Dana.

She nodded jerkily, her heart racing with fear.

"You," the man said to the clerk. "Empty the register into this bag. Hurry it up."

"Yes," the older man said, his voice trembling. "Yes, yes."

The clerk scooped out the money, dropping some on the counter, as his hands shook uncontrollably.

"Hurry up!" the man yelled.

"There," the clerk said. "That's all there is."

"You're lying, old man. Where's the safe?"

"There's no safe. This is a small town. We don't have a lot of cash to—"

"You're lying," the man hollered, his finger tightening on the trigger to the gun.

* * *

Kurt left the Hip Hop Café and stood for a moment on the sidewalk, savoring the feeling of having been well fed on a cool, clear Montana morning.

Glancing at his watch, he decided he had time to stop at the convenience store to replenish the stash of hard candy he kept in his desk at the police station.

He set off down the street at a leisurely pace, finally arriving at the store. Just as he looked at the Illinois license plate on the car in front of the store, he heard the unmistakable roar of a gun being fired.

The holdup man pulled the trigger, and the elderly man fell out of sight, to the floor behind the counter.

In the next instant, three things happened at exactly the same time.

The gunman swung the gun around in Dana's direction.

Dana Bailey flung the can of soda at him and hit him squarely between the eyes.

And Kurt Noble came barreling through the door, crouching low, gun held in both hands, just as the man dropped like a rock at Kurt's feet.

Chapter Two

J. D. Cade hoisted the last one-hundred-pound sack of feed into the bed of the pickup truck, then closed the tailgate.

Horton's Hardware and Feed Store opened early to cater to the ranchers in the area, making it possible for errands to be done shortly after dawn, so as not to disrupt a busy workday on the land.

J.D. tugged his Stetson lower, then decided a hot cup of coffee was in order before the drive back to the Kincaid ranch. He went to the passenger-side window of the truck, where a rather nondescript dog was watching him intently.

"Stay put, Freeway," J.D. said. "I won't be gone long. Stay."

The dog whined once in disapproval of the command, then flopped down on the seat, his chin on his paws.

"You can pout," J.D. said, "but you still have to stay in the truck. We'll head back to the ranch in about ten minutes."

Freeway refused to look at him. J.D. smiled for a moment at the dog's performance, then started down the sidewalk.

Head back to the ranch, his mind told him. The *Kincaid* ranch. *He* was a Kincaid, but no one in Whitehorn knew who he was, no one knew that Wayne Kincaid had not been killed in Vietnam, as they all believed.

He'd planned to just stay a few days in Whitehorn to visit his mother's grave, look the town over and attempt to put some of the ghosts of his past to rest at long last.

But now here he was, a hired hand on the spread, masquerading as J. D. Cade and trying to help out the foreman, Rand Harding, who was struggling to keep the ranch operating.

J.D. swept his gaze over the row of businesses within his view.

There had sure been a lot of changes in Whitehorn in the past twenty-five years, he mused. There were new stores, new people. And there were old memories. His parents and brother were dead and buried.

But Kate was very much alive.

Kate Randall. They had been so in love, so filled with plans for a glorious future together. They had been so damn young, honestly believing that their dreams would come true, one by one, just like they were picking apples from a tree.

But then the Vietnam war had come, and in a heartbeat everything had changed, and had never been the same again. Wayne Kincaid was believed to have died long ago in that chaos on the other side of the world, taking with him the plans for the future he and Kate dreamed about.

"So be it," J.D. said, under his breath.

Kate was married now, his mind wandered on. She was Kate Randall Walker, the wife of his best friend, Ethan. There was no point in revealing his true identity to them, or anyone else. He looked far different from the young man who had marched off to war, and no one had recognized him all these years later. It would only disrupt their lives to announce that Wayne Kincaid was living and breathing in the body he'd temporarily named J. D. Cade.

J.D. stopped on the sidewalk and frowned.

He'd been headed for the Hip Hop, but Janie Carson would no doubt be working there this morning. She was a nice young woman, very pretty, but, cripes, she fell all over him every time he entered the café.

He sure didn't want to hurt Janie's feelings, had managed to be polite, casual and *very* careful not to be overly friendly, hadn't given her any reason to think he was as interested in her as she obviously was in him.

Janie had a harmless, girlish crush on him, that was all, but he wasn't in the mood to deal with her this morning. He'd make do with a cold soda from the convenience store, instead of hot Hip Hop coffee.

J.D. smiled.

Old Clem Simmons was working part-time at the convenience store these days, for something to do with his idle hours, having long since retired from teaching. Clem had no idea that J. D. Cade, who stopped in the store now and again, was actually

Wayne Kincaid, who had soaped the windows of his house one Halloween, with his ten-year-old partner-in-crime, Travis Bains.

J.D. was pulled from his memories as he saw Kurt Noble approaching the convenience store from the opposite direction. As J.D. was about to nod a greeting, Kurt switched his attention to the license plate of a compact car parked in front of the store.

In the next instant, the sound of a gunshot reverberated through the air, shattering the peacefulness of the morning. Kurt drew his gun and barreled into the convenience store. J.D. took off at a run, arriving at the store seconds later.

She'd killed the robber, Dana thought, feeling hysteria building within her. She hadn't thought about throwing that can of soda, she'd just suddenly done it, her missile hitting the man squarely between the eyes. Dear heaven, he was dead, and she had killed him.

And look at that. The robber had a partner, who was all fancied up in a sport coat, and now *he* was pointing a gun at her. He'd shoot her, of course, because he was undoubtedly upset that she'd killed his buddy.

Oh, who was this? A cowboy? That was an authentic touch of Montana. She *was* in Montana, wasn't she? Yes, Montana, but for the life of her, she couldn't remember the name of this town.

A strange-sounding little giggle escaped from Dana's lips.

How sad, she thought. She was going to be shot to death in No Name, Montana.

* * *

Kurt took in the details of the scene with a quick, experienced scrutiny, then turned his head to see J. D. Cade entering the store.

"Check behind the counter," Kurt said to him.

J.D. hurried to do as instructed, as Kurt picked up the robber's gun from the floor. The man, who was lying on his stomach, moaned.

"Move and you won't see lunchtime," Kurt said, pointing his own gun at him.

"I'm not moving," the man said. "I'm bleeding here, cop. That damn woman broke my nose."

"Shut up," Kurt said.

"Clem is shot," J.D. said. "Looks bad." He lifted the receiver of the wall telephone behind the counter. "I'll call for an ambulance."

"Get a patrol car over here, too," Kurt said.

J.D. nodded.

Kurt pocketed the man's gun, replaced his own in its holster and unclipped the handcuffs. He pulled the man's arms behind him and clicked the cuffs into place.

"I'm bleeding to death here!" the man yelled.

"I hope so," Kurt said.

He straightened and started toward the woman, who had apparently been the one to hurl the soda can at the would-be thief.

Nice-looking lady, Kurt thought. Tall, slender, silky-looking blond hair that came to the top of her shoulders, and the biggest blue eyes he'd ever seen.

She also had a rather faraway, bemused look on her pretty face that announced she was a tad shook up over what had just happened. He'd seen that expression many times before, and he knew he had to go easy, treat her gently, talk to her quietly, until he could determine how deep her state of shock was.

"Hello," he said, smiling as he stopped in front of the woman. "I'm Kurt Noble."

"You forgot to shoot me," Dana said, then drew a wobbly breath.

Oh, boy, Kurt thought, she was right on the edge. She would either snap out of it, faint, or start to cry. Dandy. Just great.

"What's your name?" he said, still smiling.

"Me? I'm Dana Bailey. I would appreciate it, Mr. Noble, if you didn't shoot me. I certainly didn't intend to kill your partner with the soda can I threw at him. It was an accident...of sorts."

Kurt chuckled, despite his effort not to.

"Ms. Bailey...Dana..." he said, "I'm a police officer. I'm not going to shoot you. You didn't kill that sleaze, you just knocked him down. You're a heroine."

The sound of approaching vehicles with sirens wailing grew increasingly louder.

"Help is on the way," Kurt went on, "and everything is fine. Are you with me here?" He leaned forward slightly. "Dana? Hello?"

Goodness, this man, this Kurt Noble, was handsome, Dana thought foggily. Well, no, not exactly handsome, more like...ruggedly...um...compelling. Yes, that was a much better description.

His face had a lived-in look, if there was such a thing, a testament to his having been in more than one fight. But it had character, was most definitely masculine and extremely attractive. Kurt. It was a strong name, fit him to a tee. He was tall, well built, his body topped off by that intriguing face, and...

He wasn't going to shoot her? He was a police officer? Well, fancy that. She wasn't going to die in Whitehorn, Montana, after all. And she'd even remembered the name of the town she wasn't going to die in. Things were definitely looking up.

Dana took a deep breath, let it out slowly, then blinked several times.

"Well," she said, "there are mornings, and there are mornings. This one certainly wasn't run-of-the-mill, I must say."

"Welcome back," Kurt said.

"Pardon me?" Dana said.

"Never mind. Stay put, all right? I'll need to ask you some questions."

Dana nodded as Kurt strode away. She was suddenly aware that she was still holding the plastic basket containing the items she'd intended to purchase.

It seemed like a decade since she'd dropped the bottle of shampoo into the basket, she thought. How quickly and dramatically a person's life could change. Unfortunately, she'd discovered that before she ever entered the little store in Whitehorn, Montana.

An ambulance screeched to a halt outside, and seconds later a police patrol car pulled to a halt, bubble lights whirling. People began to stream into the store, the volume of noise increasing steadily.

Dana moved back, out of the way, and watched, ignoring her trembling knees and still-racing heart.

That pleasant old man had been shot, she thought. He'd come to work that morning, as he no doubt did each day, and now he was being lifted onto a stretcher, while the cowboy continued to press a blood-soaked towel to the head of the still form being buckled securely into place.

A crowd was gathering on the sidewalk, she observed, and Kurt Noble was talking to a uniformed police officer, while pointing to the people, probably giving instructions to keep everyone back.

Kurt Noble, Dana thought. She vaguely remembered taking a very thorough inventory of the man's attributes and giving him a high score out of ten. What an asinine thing to have done, in the midst of what took place there.

Dana sighed, feeing totally exhausted, as though the last ounce of energy she possessed was seeping slowly from her body, as if she were a deflating balloon.

She walked to the rear of the store, placed her basket on the floor, then leaned back against the wall. Closing her eyes, she shut out the cacophony beating against her now throbbing head.

Kurt Noble had instructed her to stay put, she thought. Okay, fine. She watched enough television to know that she'd have to give a statement to the police regarding what she had witnessed during the attempted robbery.

As a corporate attorney, she knew how to deliver a crisp, concise report, which she would do. Then she was leaving Whitehorn and the ever-increasing number of police officers around her, as quickly as possible.

Forget what her mother had taught her when she was a little girl. Dana Bailey, at twenty-eight and in the midst of her living nightmare, did not consider police officers her friends. Far from it.

She had to get out of Whitehorn before she drew any more unwanted attention to herself.

Dana opened her eyes, to see the ambulance pulling

away, the siren wailing. Kurt was shaking the hand of the cowboy, whose shirt was spattered with blood. The cowboy nodded and left the store.

Here's my chance, Dana realized. She had to get out of there, stay on the move. In the midst of all this confusion, could she just stroll out the door and drive away? It wouldn't require an official statement from *her* to document what had taken place in that convenience store.

Dana stood on tiptoe to see out the front window and inwardly groaned in frustration. Her vehicle was hemmed in by a police patrol car.

So much for the great escape.

She closed her eyes again and sighed in defeat.

"Take him in and book him," Kurt said to a uniformed officer. "Judd is in Billings today. Leave instructions at the office that he's to be told what happened if he calls in. I'll be over there shortly with the witness to have her statement taken."

"Got it," the police officer said. "Do you know how badly Clem is hurt? Man, I've known him all my life, was in his class in elementary school."

"So was I," Kurt said, running one hand over the back of his neck. "He's a decent person, who sure as hell didn't deserve this. I don't know how serious his head wound is. He was unconscious, and there was a lot of blood."

"Yeah," the officer said, frowning. "Who was that guy who tended to Clem?"

"His name is J. D. Cade," Kurt said. "Works out at the Kincaid ranch. He just jumped in and did what needed doing. He was calm and cool, like tending to a gunshot wound was all in a day's work. Let's hope that what Cade did will make a difference in how Clem comes out of this." He paused. "Get that scum out of here."

"Yep."

The handcuffed man was assisted to his feet and propelled out the door. The felon was hollering about his legal rights and demanding to see a doctor about his bleeding nose.

Kurt turned and looked for Dana Bailey, finally locating her where she stood against the back wall, her eyes closed. He walked slowly toward her.

Dana was still as pale as a ghost, he thought. She appeared done in, exhausted. Well, she'd suffered a trauma that could definitely wipe a person out. She looked vulnerable, like someone who needed a comforting hug.

Cripe, Noble, he admonished himself. Where had *that* thought come from? If he wrapped his arms around Dana Bailey's slender body...the thought of which had a certain appeal...she'd probably holler police harassment and whack him with a soda can, which was apparently her weapon of choice.

Kurt stopped about two feet in front of Dana, hoping she'd sense his presence, so that he wouldn't have to scare her to death by speaking to her, or touching her.

He waited, but Dana didn't move.

Kurt cleared his throat.

Dana's eyes flew open. "What?"

"I didn't mean to startle you," Kurt said, raising both hands. Beautiful eyes. She sure as hell had great big beautiful blue eyes. *Lord, Noble, knock it off.* "I'm sorry."

"Oh. I...I'm just very tired."

"You're coming down off an extremely high adrenaline rush, Dana. May I call you Dana? Would you like to have a doctor look you over, make certain that you're really all right?"

"No, no, I'm fine." Dana pushed away from the wall and straightened her pink string sweater over the waistband of her jeans. "I'm on a tight schedule, though, Mr. Noble, so—"

"Kurt," he said interrupting her. "We're very informal here in Whitehorn, just laid-back folks."

"Yes, well, Kurt," she said, lifting her chin, "as I was saying, I have a timetable to keep, so if I could possibly make my purchases, then give you my statement, I'll be on my way."

"I assume that is your car outside with the Illinois license plates?"

"Yes."

"Mmm…" he said, reaching down and picking up the plastic basket. "Where are you headed?"

Somewhere. Anywhere. Everywhere, Dana thought. Dear heaven, what should she say? Kurt's question was certainly reasonable. What was bizarre was that she didn't have a clue as to what the answer was.

"West," she said. "I'm going west." She smiled brightly. "Just like a pioneer of old. That's me. Heading west."

Kurt frowned as he nodded slowly. He looked at Dana for a long, studying moment, then turned and went to the refrigerator section of the store and added a can of soda to the basket. He returned to where Dana remained standing.

"I'll put this stuff in a sack for you," he said. "We're a tad short on medals, so this will be your reward from the town of Whitehorn for decking the perp and stopping the robbery.''

''Perp?'' Dana said, raising her eyebrows. ''I didn't know that police officers actually said that.''

''We say it.''

''Why aren't you in uniform? Are you a detective?''

''Yes. What do you do for a living?''

Dana moved past Kurt and answered him over her shoulder. ''I head west,'' she said, smiling pleasantly.

''Mmm...'' he said, narrowing his eyes as he followed her to the front of the store.

In the police station, Kurt produced a foam cup of coffee for Dana, then escorted her into his office. She'd followed him in her own car to the building, which was a few blocks from the convenience store.

At one point, she'd considered pressing hard on the gas pedal, whipping around a corner and fleeing. That idea had lasted approximately three seconds, as she envisioned a very angry Kurt Noble chasing her down and hauling her back to Whitehorn, demanding to know why she'd run.

While a woman's fantasies might conjure up all kinds of delicious scenarios one might engage in with the ruggedly handsome and masculinity-personified Detective Noble, having him become mad as blue blazes was not on the list of wonderful things to do.

With a sigh, Dana sank onto a hard wooden chair opposite Kurt's cluttered metal desk and took a sip of the hot, bitter coffee.

She looked up to see Kurt standing behind the desk and taking a tie from his jacket pocket. He fastened the top button of his shirt, then proceeded to secure the tie in place with a perfectly square knot.

"How did you do that without a mirror?" Dana said, cocking her head slightly to one side.

"Practice," Kurt said, sitting down. "Years of practice." He paused. "I take it that your husband—or significant other, if you'll excuse the overused term—puts his tie on in front of a mirror?"

Where had that come from? Kurt wondered. He didn't give a rip whether Dana Bailey was married or seriously involved with a man. What a corny thing to have asked her. It was lame high school dialogue, and an obvious fishing-for-personal-information question.

"I'm not married or otherwise encumbered," Dana said coolly. "I watched my father put on his tie when I was a little girl. It never failed to fascinate me. And this is a dumb conversation."

"You've got that straight," Kurt said, then hollered, "Kimberly!"

Dana jumped in her chair at Kurt's sudden outburst, nearly spilling her coffee.

"Good grief," she said, "don't you people have an intercom system here?"

"Yep," he said, grinning. "You just heard it."

The man should *not* smile, Dana thought. It softened his features and caused crinkling little lines to appear by his blue eyes. She'd felt it, the funny little flutter in the pit of her stomach when Kurt had smiled. She'd felt it, and she was totally ignoring it. She was, after all, in a weakened condition after the horrifying events she had just been subjected to.

Kurt Noble was simply a man. Well, he was an extremely attractive man, who exuded an earthy aura that shouted the message *"male"* loud and clear, but... *Oh, Dana, please shut up.*

"You rang?" a young woman said, appearing in the doorway to Kurt's office.

"Yes," Kurt said. "I need you to take a statement, please. Kim, this is Dana Bailey. Dana, Kimberly will take down the details of what took place at the store."

"Fine," Dana said.

"Do you know how Clem is doing, Kurt?" Kimberly said. "My mom had him for a teacher when she was a kid. She's going to be really upset about this."

"A lot of people are," Kurt said, "but at least we've got the perp who shot him, thanks to Dana here. And no, I don't know what condition Clem is in. Get your notebook, all right?"

"Okay," Kim said, then hurried away.

"Just take it from the top," Kurt said to Dana, "but go slowly, because Kim doesn't know shorthand."

"Then why is she the one taking statements?"

Kurt shrugged. "Beats me. You'd have to ask Sheriff Hensley that. Judd does the hiring and firing around this place."

"A sheriff is in charge of the police, rather than a police chief?"

"Strange, but true," Kurt said. "We have police officers on duty in Whitehorn, and deputy sheriffs on duty outside the city limit, into the county. Judd is in charge of the whole deal, and we overlap our territories, don't pay any attention to the county or city lines."

"Weird."

"I suppose it is, but it's always been that way. Then there's the res, which has its own police force.

We have to get permission to go in there in an official capacity.''

"The res?"

"The Laughing Horse Indian Reservation."

"I'm back," Kim said, rushing into the room. "Kurt, Judd is on line one for you."

Kurt got to his feet. "I'll take it outside. You two get started."

Kimberly watched Kurt leave the office, and Dana watched Kim watching Kurt.

"He's dreamy," the young girl said, looking at Dana again. "Well, for an old guy, he's pretty sexy."

"Old?" Dana said, raising her eyebrows. "He looks about thirty-five maybe thirty-six."

Kimberly nodded. "Right. Old. Okay, here we go. Tell me everything that happened."

Dana sighed. "I parked in front of the convenience store, and…"

"Got it," Kurt said into the receiver of the telephone. "I'll tell you this, though, Judd—Dana Bailey is *not* going to be happy with this newsflash…. No, I don't know why she's in Whitehorn, or exactly where she's headed. She's been dancing around answering those kinds of questions. But she did make it clear that she was in a hurry to be on her way…. Yeah, I understand. I know we can, and I'll make that clear to her. When are you coming in? Okay, I'll see you then…. What? No, I'm going to call the hospital now and find out how Clem is doing. Yep. Yep. See ya."

Kurt replaced the receiver, looked up the number for the hospital, then spoke to a high-ranking nurse. The call completed, he went back into his office, just as Kimberly was getting to her feet.

"I'll type this in triplicate and you can sign it," Kimberly said to Dana.

"Will it take long?" Dana said.

"Well, I'm not a very fast typist, but I'll do it as quickly as I can." Kimberly started toward the door. "Hi, Kurt. Did you phone the hospital?"

Kurt nodded. "Clem is in a deep coma. The bullet caught him alongside the head. They're not predicting anything about his chances at this point."

"I'd better call my mom and let her know the latest about Clem."

"But you're going to type my statement," Dana said, shifting in the chair to look at Kimberly.

"Oh, I will," she said, "just as soon as I finish talking to my mother."

Dana got to her feet, dropped the empty cup in the trash can and began to wander restlessly around the small office.

Kurt moved past her and sank onto the creaking leather chair behind his desk.

"Chicago," he said. "Illinois license plates and big-city hurry-up attitude. I've got five bucks that says you're from Chicago."

Dana stopped her trek and frowned. "Does it matter where I'm from?"

"I'm just being friendly. Chatting. Making small talk."

"I don't have time to chat, Detective Noble. I must be on my way."

Kurt ran one hand over his chin. "Well, I was just speaking to Sheriff Hensley about that. You know, the fact that you're apparently in a rush to be hitting the road."

"And?"

"Why don't you sit down?"

"No, thank you," Dana said.

"Whatever. Anyway, Judd said I was to inform you that your presence is required here in Whitehorn as a witness in the trial of the perp who shot Clem."

"What?"

"In other words, Ms. Bailey, you can't leave town."

Chapter Three

Hearing Kurt Noble's unbelievable statement Dana felt panic sweep through her like a chilling current. Her first instinct was to bolt. By sheer force of will, she reined in her fear and allowed the emotion that followed to come to the fore.

Anger.

She marched to the front of Kurt's desk, planted her hands flat on the cluttered top and leaned toward him.

"You," she said, her voice quivering with fury, "are out of your tiny mind, mister."

Sensational, Kurt thought. Dana Bailey mad as hell was really something to behold. Her big blue eyes were flashing laser beams, her cheeks were flushed, her silky hair was swinging, beckoning to his hands to sift his fingers through it.

She was so close to him. All he had to do was lean

forward a bit, and he could capture those enticing lips of Dana's with his own. Her lush breasts were straining against her sweater, and the fair skin of her slender throat looked like soft white velvet. Oh, yeah, she was definitely sensational.

Yes, indeed, Kurt thought, this was one fantastic woman, and that realization was causing heat to coil tight and low in his body.

"Goodbye, Detective Noble," Dana said, straightening. "It has *not* been a pleasure meeting you."

"Hold it," Kurt said, getting to his feet. He came around the desk to stand directly in front of Dana. "I wasn't kidding, you know. I have orders from Sheriff Hensley to inform you that a subpoena will be issued saying you're to testify at the perp's trial, and that you're to remain in Whitehorn until said trial takes place."

"You can't do that!" Dana said, nearly shrieking, as she planted her hands on her hips. "This is a free country. You can't hold me here against my will.

"I gave you my statement regarding what I witnessed during the attempted robbery. That man is as guilty as sin. You know it, I know it, and a jury will know it. I've met my obligations as a good little citizen, and I'm leaving. Right now."

Kurt shook his head. "A statement read in court, or even a videotaped one that is shown to the jury, doesn't do the job we want it to. It leaves a loophole, too big a risk of the perp getting off, because the defense attorney can't cross-examine you."

"Tough."

"Dana, come on. There's a decent human being, a kind old man, fighting for his life in the hospital at this very minute. You're the guarantee that we can put the guy who shot Clem behind bars for a very long time. Doesn't that mean anything to you? Do you want that scum to walk, not pay for what he did to Clem?''

"No, of course not," she said wearily, wrapping her hands around her elbows, "but you don't understand. I'm not on vacation, just meandering across the country at a leisurely pace, stopping as the mood strikes. I have important business to attend to."

"Where?"

"Not here!"

Kurt frowned. "What's the big secret about your destination? And if you're in such an all-fired hurry, why aren't you on the main freeway? Whitehorn is way off the beaten track, you know."

"Detective Noble," Dana said, narrowing her eyes, "I am not on the witness stand. I don't have to answer your questions regarding my personal agenda."

"Fine. You can be as closemouthed as you want to be, but you're *not* leaving Whitehorn."

"You can't do this."

"Yes, Ms. Bailey, I can."

Dana and Kurt glared at each other, the tension in the room nearly crackling with its intensity.

Blue eyes met blue eyes.

Bodies were stiff and tight with anger and frustration.

Then, slowly, very slowly, something shifted. Changed. The cold fury was pushed aside by a heat that began to thrum in the body of man, in the body of woman.

It was the heat of desire, causing hearts to race and the room to disappear into a haze of passion-laden mist, that swirled around them. Hot. So hot.

"Kurt?" Dana whispered.

"Dana, I..." he began, his voice raspy.

Dana blinked and took a step backward.

"No," she said, then drew a steadying breath. She lifted her chin. "Does that usually work for you, Kurt? Have you practiced your seduction routine as often as you've practiced putting on your tie without a mirror?

"Well, you've got the wrong woman this time. I'm not falling prey to your oh-so-sexy gaze from your gorgeous blue eyes. I outgrew falling for that malarkey when I was Kimberly's age."

"What in the hell are you talking about?" Kurt said, none too quietly. "*I'm* not the one with the biggest blue eyes in the western hemisphere. Eyes that could melt metal if you put your mind to it. Well, listen up, lady. You're not wiggling out of your humanitarian *and* legal duty in Whitehorn by turning on your womanly wiles."

"You," Dana said, nearly sputtering with anger, "are despicable."

"And you are coming across as self-centered and selfish. You're the one who can put behind bars the man who shot Clem, and, by damn, you're going to do it."

"But I can't stay here. I...I have a sick aunt who needs me." Dana pointed one finger in the air. "Yes, she's desperately ill, and I'm rushing to her bedside. How will you live with the guilt if you hold me here and my grandmother—no, no, my aunt—dies?"

"Want to toss in a sick uncle and grandfather for good measure?" Kurt said dryly. He shook his head, then went back around his desk and sat down. "I'll make some calls and find you a place to stay. The town of Whitehorn will pick up the tab.''

''I don't believe this,'' Dana said, sinking onto the wooden chair.

Dear heaven, this was crazy, she thought frantically. She was being detained by the police in Whitehorn, Montana, who had no idea she was being sought by the police in Chicago, Illinois. How was she going to prove her innocence if she was stuck in this dinky town? The nightmare that was her life was becoming worse by the minute.

''Kurt,'' she said, striving for pleasant and friendly, ''I'll come back for the trial and testify my little heart out.''

''Oh?'' he said, raising one eyebrow. ''Come back from where?''

''Wherever I am. I'll... Yes, I'll call you every few days, and the minute you need me to testify—'' Dana snapped her fingers ''—I'll pop right up.''

''No.''

''Kurt, please, I...''

''No.''

''I'm going to call my attorney.'' Dana sighed. ''That was brilliant, Dana. I *am* my attorney.''

''You're a lawyer?''

''Yes.''

''Then you ought to know that what I'm doing by subpoenaing you and requiring you to stay put is perfectly legal.''

''I'm a corporate attorney. I probably covered nonsense like this in a class in college, but if I did, I don't remember.''

''Well, trust me, I'm operating within the law.'' Kurt lifted the receiver to the telephone. ''I'll see if

there's a room available at the Amity Boardinghouse.
That's a nice place.''

Trust me, Dana's mind echoed, as she tuned out
Kurt's conversation on the telephone. She didn't have
the luxury of trusting Kurt Noble. The only people
she had any faith in at the moment were Todd Gunderson, back in her Chicago office, and the detective
she'd hired. She had to view everyone else as a potential enemy.

Dana shifted her gaze to Kurt, who was doodling
on a piece of paper as he talked on the telephone.

Trust him? she thought. Not a chance. He was a
badge-carrying officer of the law. Not only that, but
after the strange sensual spell he'd cast over her for
those passion-laden moments, she'd do well to not
trust *herself* around Kurt Noble. The man was potent,
had caused desire to flash through her like a brushfire.

If she actually had to stay in Whitehorn—and it
appeared she had no choice in the matter—she wasn't
going within ten feet of Detective Noble for the duration. He was trouble in a six-foot masculine package, and she had enough on her plate to deal with.

"Okay," Kurt said, replacing the receiver and
snapping Dana back to attention. "The Amity is having the rooms painted, so I've booked you into the
Whitehorn Motel, on the edge of town. It's nothing
fancy, but it's clean." He got to his feet. "Let's go.
I'll get you settled in."

"I'm perfectly capable of settling in on my own,
thank you," Dana said stiffly.

Kurt smiled. "It's all part of the service, ma'am.
We aim to please here in Whitehorn."

Kurt Noble, Dana thought, getting to her feet,
should *not* be allowed to smile. Why didn't they make

that against the law? It would be just as ridiculous as the legality that was keeping her here against her will, like a crummy common criminal.

Oh, Lord, she thought in the next instant. There were a whole slew of people in Chicago who believed that was exactly the title she deserved to have.

The Whitehorn Motel was old and, despite a fairly recent coat of bright yellow paint, looked its age. It consisted of an office and a long single row of fifteen rooms, edged at the end by woods.

Kurt had made reservations for Dana in the last room, telling her it would afford her privacy and quiet.

"Whatever," she said, as he unlocked the door to the room.

Dana placed her suitcase on the double bed and glanced around.

It was no better, or worse, than the places she'd been staying in since she fled Chicago, she thought.

The room held an odor of cleaning solvent, the furnishings were basically green, including faded carpet and a wash-worn bedspread. There was a small television bolted to the top of a dresser, as well as a minuscule chair and table and one lamp.

Kurt peered into the bathroom.

"Spit-shined and pretty," he said.

Dana sank onto the edge of the bed with a sigh as a wave of utter exhaustion swept over her.

She was so tired, she thought. Of everything. This incident in Whitehorn was the crowning blow, was threatening to be the straw that would topple her fragile tower of courage.

Somehow, *somehow*, she had to reach within herself even deeper than before, for the determination to keep going, to not rest, *not cry,* until she'd proved her innocence.

But, oh, God, it was all so frightening, and she was so terribly alone.

Kurt frowned as he stared at Dana. Her head was bent, and her hands were clutched tightly in her lap.

She seemed to have forgotten he was there, Kurt thought. It was as though she were beginning to crumble, was hanging on by a thread.

Dana Bailey was a mystery waiting to be unraveled. Either she was a very private person, who refused to share her personal business with a stranger, or she had something to hide.

Why wouldn't she tell him where she was headed and why she was going there? What was the big secret?

No, now wait a minute. That was the detective in him mentally squinting his eyes at Dana's unwillingness to be forthcoming with information. If he forgot the badge and viewed her simply as a man, he'd have to admit it was none of his business what she was doing this far from Illinois.

View her simply as a man, Kurt's mind echoed. The man was seeing a woman who looked so exhausted, vulnerable and forlorn, it was enough to make his gut ache.

The man was seeing a lovely woman, so damn pretty in a natural way, without benefit of gobs of makeup.

The man was seeing a woman who had caused desire to coil hot and low in his body during that eerie moment in his office.

"Look," Kurt said, "why don't you get some rest?

You're beat, which is certainly understandable, considering what you've been through this morning.''

Dana nodded, but continued to stare at her hands.

"I know that Judd—the sheriff—will push for a trial to be held as quickly as possible," Kurt went on. "We'll do everything within our power to get you on your way as fast as we can."

Dana nodded again.

"Whitehorn is a nice little town, with friendly people. You just might enjoy your stay here, if you give it a chance, and... Hell.''

Kurt looked up at the ceiling for a long moment before redirecting his attention to Dana.

"Dana, I know this stinks, and I'm sorry. You're one of the good guys, and you're being treated like one of the bad guys. Maybe you can find some comfort in the fact that folks around here are going to be very grateful that your testimony will convict the slime that shot Clem. As my niece, Chloe, would say, you should have warm fuzzies about what you're doing.''

Kurt muttered an earthy expletive.

"Noble,'' he said, "that was one of the dumbest things you've ever said.''

Dana raised her head slowly and met Kurt's gaze, causing him to nearly groan aloud when he saw the bleak expression on her face and the fatigue in her big blue eyes.

"Ah, Dana...''

Before he realized he'd moved, Kurt closed the distance between them, gripped Dana's upper arms gently and drew her up into his embrace. He wrapped his arms around her, and she encircled his back with her own arms, leaning her head on his shoulder.

Kurt inhaled Dana's aroma of soap and fresh air, and savored the sensation of her silky hair whispering against his cheek. He was acutely aware of her lush breasts pressing against his chest, and the fact that she fit the contours of his body as though she'd been custom-made just for him.

"My sister, Leigh," he said, his voice slightly gritty, "says a hug can solve a multitude of things. She has two kids, who are six and eight years old, and sometimes she says to Max or Chloe, 'You look like someone who needs a hug.' Whichever one it is goes flying right into her arms, and I swear they feel better for it. I've seen it work."

Kurt tightened his hold on Dana.

"Dana Bailey," he said, "you look like someone who needs a hug, so that's what I'm doing."

Dana closed her eyes, blanked her mind and allowed the wondrous warm comfort of Kurt's strong arms and tall, solid body to suffuse her. She was giving herself permission to lean on him, both physically and emotionally, just for a minute. And, oh, dear heaven, it felt so good.

For this stolen tick of time, she wasn't frightened, because she was held in the safe cocoon of Kurt Noble's arms. Nor was she alone, because Kurt was there.

He smelled so good, she thought rather hazily, like fresh air, and sunshine and man. His chest was a hard wall, his arms were powerful, yet tempered with gentleness.

This was a cop with a gun, who was also a man who knew about warm fuzzies and comforting hugs.

She'd remember this moment, draw strength from

this moment, and she was now going to thank Kurt from the bottom of her heart for this moment.

Dana raised her head to express her gratitude to Kurt for his kindness and caring, but no words came as her breath caught.

Her lips were only inches from his. He was close, so close, and was looking directly into her eyes, his own radiating desire in its purest form.

Dana, step away, her mind screamed. Kurt was going to kiss her, she knew he was, and she mustn't allow that to happen.

Dana didn't move.

Don't do it, Noble, Kurt ordered himself. He was going to release his hold on Dana right now, and erase the image in his mind of his lips capturing her enticing lips. Yes, he was going to let her go. *Right now.*

Kurt didn't move.

And his mouth melted over Dana's.

He parted her lips to slip his tongue into the sweet darkness of her mouth, and she met his tongue boldly with her own, stroking, dueling.

Desire exploded within them, hot and swirling, then pulsing low in an ever-increasing tempo. Their hearts raced wildly, and their labored breathing echoed in the stark, quiet room.

Kurt lifted his head a fraction of an inch to draw a rough breath, then slanted his mouth in the other direction as he reclaimed the lips eagerly seeking his.

It was ecstasy.

It was torment.

It was a kiss that held a promise of more, of bodies meshing into one entity, of bursting upon the place where exquisite release waited to welcome them.

Noble, a niggling little voice in Kurt's mind said,

this woman may very well have secrets, should not be automatically trusted. You should not be kissing Dana Bailey.

Kurt broke the kiss and stepped back so abruptly that Dana teetered, then plunked down on the bed. She pressed one hand to her racing heart, then looked up at Kurt, startled to see that he appeared angry.

"That was a mistake," he said, his voice thick with lingering passion. He pointed a finger at Dana. "That will *not* happen again."

Dana narrowed her eyes. "I don't care for your tone of voice, Detective Noble, nor for your accusing finger in front of my face. You seem to be insinuating that what just happened between us was entirely my fault."

Kurt swept his coat back and planted his hands on his narrow hips—a gesture so blatantly male that Dana felt a warm flush of lingering heat stain her cheeks.

"You didn't exactly push me away," Kurt said, his voice rising. "You returned my kisses, Ms. Bailey, with a great deal of enthusiasm."

"I don't deny that. I also agree that it was a mistake and will not happen again. However, you're as much to blame here as I am."

"Yeah, I know," he said, raking one hand through his hair.

"Fine. Then we're in agreement, due to communicating on the subject matter. We were equal partners in an...an episode that was executed by poor judgment and won't be repeated."

"You sound really snooty when you get in your attorney mode, do you know that?"

Dana jumped to her feet. "And you sound like a

character in a bad movie when you use jargon like *perp.* I'm talking *really* corny. *Perp.* Jeez.''

They stood there glowering at each other, and then a slow smile began to inch across Kurt's lips until it grew into a full-blown grin.

''Well,'' he said, starting toward the door, ''snooty lawyer or not, you sure are one hell of a fine kisser.''

''You're not too shabby yourself,'' Dana said, laughing, ''Sergeant Friday.''

Kurt stopped, his hand on the doorknob. The flicker of merriment was gone as quickly as it had come.

''I'll check in with you later,'' he said quietly, not one hint of the smile remaining on his face. ''Kimberly ought to have your statement ready sometime today, even as slow as she types. I'll bring it out here for you to sign. If you need anything, you know where I am.''

Dana wrapped her hands around her elbows. ''Yes. Fine. Thank you.''

Kurt strode back across the room and scribbled on a pad of paper by the telephone.

''That's my home phone number,'' he said.

Dana nodded.

Kurt started toward the door again, stopped, then returned to stand in front of Dana. He framed her face in his hands, dipped his head and kissed her; it was a toe-curling, breath-stealing kiss.

When he finally released her, Dana stared at him with wide eyes.

''What—?'' She drew much-needed air into her lungs. ''What on earth was that for?''

''That,'' Kurt said, his brows knit in a frown, ''was because kisses like the ones we've shared shouldn't be analyzed and talked to death the way we did. Because kisses like those don't come waltzing down the pike every day of the week.''

"Oh. Well, I—"

"Shh. Leave that last kiss alone." He nodded decisively. "Just leave it be. I'll see you later on, Dana."

Kurt spun around and left the room. Dana stared at the door he'd closed behind him. It was several minutes before she realized that the fingertips of one hand had floated up to rest on her tingling lips, which held the lingering taste of Kurt Noble.

Kurt drove at a crawl, not wishing to return immediately to the noise and confusion at the police station. He turned onto a quiet side street, still keeping well below the speed limit.

When he was shot, he thought with self-disgust, the doctors had somehow missed the fact that his brain had been damaged by the bullet that tore into his shoulder.

What had taken place in that motel room with Dana Bailey was so insane, it was a crime. He had to be partially brain-dead to have done such an asinine thing.

Dana was a witness to a crime, and he was the police officer in charge of the case. Everything should have been kept on a professional level, strictly business.

Hadn't he learned a damn thing from what happened in Seattle? Hadn't he promised himself, once he realized he was going to live after hovering near death after being shot, that he would never again, *never,* allow his emotions to rule his actions? Oh, yeah, he'd made that vow, and meant every word of it.

Kurt smacked the steering wheel with the heel of his left hand, then stifled a groan as pain radiated up his arm and across his chest.

So what did he do, despite his sworn oath to himself? he mentally raged on. The very first time he encountered a woman who was connected to his job, a woman who tugged at his heart with her vulnerability and her sad blue eyes, he hauled her into his arms and kissed her socks off.

"Damn," he muttered.

And as if that weren't bad enough in itself, Dana had secrets, was hiding something, continually danced wide circles around the truth of where she was going and why.

In Seattle, he'd been suckered by a woman who was not who she appeared to be. She'd played him like a fiddle under her command, and he'd been jerked around to whatever tune she wished to hear at the moment. He'd been a fool in spades, and it had nearly cost him his life.

Well, not this time, by damn. He was pulling back, regrouping, taking charge of his feeble brain. He was staying away, far away, from Dana.

He'd send Kimberly to the motel to get Dana's signature on the typed statement. Yes, that was a good idea. Kim, or even Judd, could then keep their star witness informed on the progress being made toward setting a trial date for the scum who had shot Clem.

Okay, now he was cooking, was back in control. Dana would be out of sight, out of mind, just someone stashed in a motel on the edge of town until her testimony was required in court.

Fine.

Kurt frowned as he turned the vehicle around, with the intention of going back to the station.

There was just one glitch in his master plan, he thought. How in the hell was he going to forget the way Dana had nestled perfectly against him? How was he going to forget her aroma, the silky strands of her golden hair, the sweet taste of her lips as they'd responded in abandon to his own?

How was he going to forget how much he wanted to make love with Dana Bailey?

Chapter Four

The citizens of Whitehorn and beyond woke the next morning to a chilly, steady rain that had begun to fall during the night. The heavy clouds in the heavens were gunmetal gray, without one hint of blue sky managing to peek through.

J. D. Cade wore a yellow slicker as he rode fence on the Kincaid ranch, checking for any problems in the miles of barbed wire.

Many ranch hands hated this chore, he knew. They found it tedious and boring, and far too isolated. But during the years he was a prisoner of war, he'd learned how to be totally and absolutely alone. He'd learned, because the alternative would have been to go out of his mind, to slip into the world of insanity.

J.D. nudged his horse, urging it to go faster. He squinted and leaned forward in the saddle, attempting to determine exactly what he was seeing a hundred yards down the fence line.

At the spot he'd been concentrating on, J.D. pulled on the reins to halt the horse, then swung out of the saddle. A deep frown knit his brows as he stared at the fence.

There were six dead chickens hanging from the barbed wire, having been tied in place with strips of leather.

J.D. swore under his breath.

Who in the hell had done this? he wondered. Lord, he hated the idea of having to tell Rand Harding that there was another incident to report to the sheriff.

The list of malicious pranks was growing larger, and J.D. was becoming angrier with every one that was added to the tally.

Rand was having difficulty keeping hands on the payroll, as many of the drifters coming through came to believe the rumors that the Kincaid spread was haunted by ghosts.

Dead chickens hanging from barbed wire were not going to help the unrest and edginess among the men.

Why? J.D. thought, getting back on his horse. Why was someone doing all this rotten stuff? What did they hope to gain?

Whoever was behind it was clever and methodical. There was nothing haphazard about the way those chickens were hung on the fence. They were spaced exactly the same distance apart, and the head of each was draped over the top wire.

When word of this latest bizarre happening reached the ranch hands, how many would quit? The rumors would be fanned by fear, the chickens seen as some sort of ghostly ritual that was sending the message to get off of Kincaid land.

Well, by damn, Wayne Kincaid wasn't leaving, he thought. Not yet. He wanted answers. He wanted the guilty party behind this horrendous scheme caught and made to explain the motive.

No, he wasn't leaving. He'd keep on being J. D. Cade until this sick mystery was solved and the Kincaid ranch was restored to the fine Montana spread it had once been. The ranch belonged to baby Jennifer McCallum now, and she deserved to inherit the place in the shape it should be in.

Thunder rumbled through the dark clouds, and a jagged streak of lightning lit up the sky.

"Damn," J.D. said.

He'd have to seek shelter, instead of going directly back to report what he'd found. He was a sitting duck to be hit by lightning on the open range, a fact every cowboy was taught early on. He had no desire to end up as dead as one of those chickens.

Another weather front must have rolled in, he thought, bringing thunder and lightning to add to the pouring rain. He could only hope it would pass on through the area as quickly as it had come.

J.D. turned his horse and flicked the reins, causing the large animal to leap forward in a gallop.

He'd go to the cave, J.D. thought. The same cave where he'd played as a boy and sought shelter from storms.

The same cave where he'd gone at times just to be alone, during the turbulent years of his adolescence.

The same cave where later he and Kate Randall had been together on more than one occasion, making love and making plans for their future together, putting into words, as if they were weaving a beautiful tapestry, the dreams of all they would share.

Forget it, J.D. thought.

He yanked his Stetson farther down on his forehead as the horse pounded across the muddy ground.

There was nothing to be gained by looking back, he thought, going through a mental if-only list. During the war and the years that followed, he'd come to live in the present, not dwelling on the past or dreaming about the future. He simply existed in the moment at hand.

And this moment, he thought, glancing up quickly at the sky, could very well be his last, if he didn't get out of the line of fire of the ever-increasing lightning.

The sprawl of large rocks fronted by a grove of trees that J.D. was headed for came into blurry view through the downpour. Passing through a grouping of tall trees during an electrical storm was dangerous as hell, but there was no choice. He had to pass through the trees to get to the sought-after cave.

At the edge of the wooded area, J.D. pulled the horse to a stop and dropped to the ground.

"I don't need to risk your neck, fella," J.D. said, patting the animal's neck. "Head for the barn." He smacked the horse on the rump. "Go. Go home, boy. Barn. Go to the barn."

The horse snorted, pawed the ground once, then raced away in the direction J.D. had ordered him to go. J.D. darted into the trees and ran toward where he knew the cave would be, offering shelter, and a big serving of memories that he'd refuse to indulge in.

The wind had picked up, whipping the branches of the trees into a frenzied dance that was accompanied by swirling, cold rain and the thunder and lightning. Hardly able to see three feet in front of him, J.D. ran with instincts on full alert, mentally envisioning the location of the cave.

Twenty more feet, he thought, his heart pounding. Then up and over two big boulders, veer to the left, climb three small rocks then...bingo...the cave. One nice thing about caves...no one could pick 'em up and move 'em. It would still be there, just as it always had been.

J.D. broke free of the trees, was up and over the big boulders, headed left, then scrambled his way up the smaller rocks. The rocks were slippery and his boots muddy, and he lost his footing on the last rock. He felt himself being propelled forward and automatically shot his arms out to break his fall.

He hit the ground with a thud that knocked the wind out of him, then literally slid headfirst on his belly into the cave, his wet slicker acting like a sleek sled on snow. He came to a sudden and jarring halt as his body encountered the dry earth inside the cave.

"Damn it to hell," he said, gasping for breath.

"Tsk, tsk," a female voice said. "Is that any kind of proper language to use when you come calling on a lady, cowboy?"

J.D.'s head snapped up, and his heart seemed to skip a beat before starting to thunder in his chest as he stared at the scene before him.

A small fire was burning with beckoning warmth near the back wall of the cave, and behind it a woman sat cross-legged on the ground.

A woman who was smiling at him.

A woman who was causing images from the past,

vivid memories, to slam against his mind in painful and rapid succession.

A woman who had once been his purpose, his focus, his raison d'être, the other half of the very essence of himself, making him whole.

Kate.

She laughed, and the sound, the wind-chime sound, caused J.D. to close his eyes for a moment, savoring the lilting resonance.

Kate.

Get a grip, Kincaid, J.D. thought frantically. He'd known he'd see Kate eventually. It was inevitable in a town the size of Whitehorn. But, oh, Lord, why did it have to be here in the cave where they'd planned their future together, made love together, dreamed together?

"Hello?" Kate said, smiling. "Are you asleep down there?" She frowned in the next instant. "Goodness, you're not hurt, are you? You really landed hard when you came flying in here."

"No, no, I'm fine," J.D. said, pushing himself up to a sitting position. "I just had the wind knocked out of me, that's all."

"Well, come by the fire and get warm. Oh, I should introduce myself. I'm Kate Randall Walker."

J.D. pulled off the dripping slicker, using the moments to gather his composure. He stood, remembering to bend over slightly to avoid whacking his head on the top of the enclosure. He moved to where Kate was and sat down opposite the fire, sitting Indian-style, as she was.

"J. D. Cade," he said, looking at Kate intently. "I work on the Kincaid spread."

"Ah," Kate said, nodding.

She wouldn't recognize his voice, J.D. knew. When he was a prisoner of war, he'd had a throat infection that went untreated for a very long time, leaving his voice deeper, more gravelly. And heaven knew he no longer even remotely resembled the Wayne Kincaid who had gone off to the war.

But Kate? The years had been good to her. She looked older, of course, but the maturity was becoming. She was still a very beautiful woman. In the glow of the firelight, she was, in fact, exquisite, absolutely lovely.

Knock it off, Kincaid, he admonished himself. He'd do well to remember how Kate had introduced herself. She was Kate Randall Walker. *Walker.* She was married to his best friend, Ethan.

And she'd had Ethan's baby.

"So," Kate said, "what were you doing out on the range on this rainy morning?"

"Riding fence," J.D. said. Kate had been riding in the rain because she always enjoyed doing that, said it was peaceful and relaxing. "And you?"

"I love to ride in the rain. I know it sounds crazy, but I find it very relaxing. When the lightning appeared, though, I had to head for cover." She cocked her head slightly to one side, in a gesture that was achingly familiar to J.D. "How on earth did you know this cave was here? You're obviously new to the area, and this place can't be easily seen."

"Rand Harding, the foreman at the ranch, pointed it out to me when we were riding this way a while back. He wanted me to know it was here in case something happened like today's weather."

"Good thinking." Kate paused. "It's a strange feeling to realize that my life was in danger out there and the moment I stepped inside this cave I was safe again.''

"Mmm.''

"I felt as though I was moving in slow motion when I was trying to get to the cave,'' Kate went on. "I admit that I was terribly frightened. I kept thinking about my husband, Ethan, his niece, Darcy, who is like a daughter to us, our Twiglet. And, of course, our precious baby boy, Wayne.''

"You named...'' J.D. cleared his throat. "You named your son Wayne?''

"Yes. Wayne Ethan Walker. He's so adorable. He's just starting to walk, and wobbles like a drunken sailor. He looks just like Ethan.'' Kate laughed. "I can't see any resemblance to me in Wayne at all, even though I did have a great deal to do with him being here. He's his daddy's son, head to toe.''

"You named him Ethan after his father.''

"Yes, and Wayne for a very dear friend of Ethan's and mine, who was killed in Vietnam. We all grew up together, you see.''

"That's a very big honor you've given your friend, Wayne. I'm sure he'd be pleased.''

"I like to think he knows...somehow,'' Kate said. "So tell me, Mr. Cade, what does J.D. stand for?''

J.D. shrugged. "Nothing.''

"Your parents actually gave you initials for a name? How unusual.''

"I've never given it much thought, I guess. I just am who I am.''

Kate looked at him for such a long moment that J.D. pulled his gaze from hers and stared into the flames of the little fire.

"Yes,'' Kate said finally. "You are who you are.''

J.D. looked up at her quickly, studying her expression, attempting to garner a clue to what she meant by the softly spoken words. Kate's face revealed nothing.

"Where do you come from, J.D.?" Kate asked.

"Here and there. Does your little boy talk yet?"

"He says a few words," Kate said, smiling. "Some are very clear. He can say *doggy, cookie,* and a resounding *no.* Other words are only understood by Ethan, Darcy and me. Darcy adores her baby brother. I'm filled with such joy when I watch them play together, and..."

"J.D., you are a glutton for punishment. You're held captive in this cave, and you're egging on a happy and proud wife and mother to talk about her family."

"Well, it's like you said," J.D. said. "Our lives were in danger outside, in that storm. We could have been struck by lightning as easily as not. Having just experienced that, it's good to hear about a happy family, people with...with dreams."

"Dreams," Kate said, a rather wistful tone to her voice. "Sometimes they get shattered, destroyed by events beyond one's control. A person then has to make a choice. They can hold on to the fragments, which means they really have nothing, or they can move forward, look to the future and embrace new dreams. Don't you agree?"

"Yes."

"You have to know when to let go of the past," Kate said. She lifted her gaze and met his. "Let the broken dreams rest in peace."

My God, J.D. thought, his heart racing, *Kate knows.* She knew who he was, he was certain of it. She knew she was sitting by the warming fire in the memory-filled cave with Wayne Kincaid.

And in her own gentle, wise and wonderful way, she was letting him know she forgave him for not returning to her after the war.

Ah, Kate. Beautiful Kate.

She was happy with Ethan and their children. There was a serene aura about her, a sense of grace and peace.

So be it.

He wished her well. He wished for happiness and sunshine to surround her for the remainder of her days. Now he, too, might be able to allow the fragments of his dreams to rest easy. Maybe.

"Hello in the cave!" a man yelled.

"That's Rand," J.D. said, rolling to his feet and turning toward the opening to the cave. "My horse must have made it back to the barn, and the electrical storm must have passed on through."

"My horse will wander around eating like she's at a Sunday brunch," Kate said, laughing. "I was in for a long walk home. Do you think the Kincaid ranch will provide taxi service for me?"

J.D. looked back at her over his shoulder.

"Yes," he said quietly, "as a representative of the Kincaid spread, I'll guarantee that you'll be delivered safely home to your family."

"Thank you…J.D.," Kate said softly.

"No, I'm the one thanking you, Kate."

He turned to face her fully, and they looked at each other in the glow of the firelight for a long moment, a last moment. Then J.D. spun around, bent over slightly, and went to the entrance of the cave to holler a greeting to Rand Harding.

* * *

Late that afternoon, Dana was pacing back and forth in the motel room as far as the telephone cord would allow.

"You haven't found one trace of Natalie?" she said into the receiver.

"No, not so far," a man said. "She seems to have disappeared into thin air."

"So the police are still looking for *me*."

"I'm afraid so. Listen, I'm not giving up. You hired the best detective in these parts—me—to find your twin sister, and I intend to do exactly that. Natalie is somewhere. I think she's being hidden by the people who hired her. That would make sense. It will also make it more difficult to find her."

Dana pressed one hand to her forehead as a stress headache began to throb.

"Why won't the police believe me when I tell them that I would never do anything to jeopardize a career that I worked so hard for, am totally dedicated to. It was Natalie who did this, not me. We're identical twins. She was impersonating me, and—"

"I know, I know. But it's like I told you before, since you can't produce Natalie, it sounds like a pretty far-fetched story. We've covered all this, Dana."

Dana sighed. "I realize that, Mr. Parker. I'm sorry for complaining like this."

"Pete. You're supposed to call me Pete."

"Yes, of course...Pete. Oh, dear, everything is in such a mess. I'm stuck here in Whitehorn, Montana, for heaven only knows how long. As the major witness to the robbery attempt at the store, I'm practically glued to the police department. Can you believe this? It couldn't get any worse." She paused. "Have you spoken recently with Todd Gunderson at my office?''

''Yeah, I checked in with him yesterday. He's really worried about you. I hope you realize the guy is nuts about you.

''Anyway, he said that the big shot who put in the buy order for the stock is out on bail. His attorney is going to cop a plea, present him as an innocent bystander who was approached by you with insider-trading information to sell regarding the merger of those two companies.

''The only thing he's guilty of, they're claiming, is being greedy. The down and dirty is falling directly on your head.''

''It was Natalie who did it all!'' Dana said, nearly shrieking.

''But they have witnesses who saw *you* in the office late the night before the buy order went in the next morning. You were also seen outside the building, getting into a car belonging to the guy they snagged.''

''Yes, I know,'' Dana said wearily. ''I was home in bed with a bad cold that night. Natalie said she would go to the store to get me some juice. She never came back. Oh, Pete, how am I going to prove my innocence if we can't find my sister?''

''I'll find her. You sit tight.'' Pete chuckled. ''Not that you have any choice in the matter. That's what you get for being Wonder Woman during the robbery attempt.

''Well, look at the bright side, Dana. I now have a telephone number where I can reach you if something breaks, instead of having to wait to hear from you.''

"Good grief, is that all you can come up with for a bright side?"

"At the moment? Yes. But I'm giving this my best shot. You'll have to be patient. Remember…everyone is somewhere, and I'm very good at finding the person I'm looking for."

A knock sounded at the motel door.

"There's someone at my door," Dana said. "I've got to go. You'll call me the minute you have any leads on where Natalie is? Keep me completely informed? Even the smallest bit of information will give me something to hold on to. All right?"

"You bet. Try to relax, if you possibly can. There's nothing you can do at your end but wait. I'll stay in touch."

The knock sounded again.

"Yes, okay. Thank you, Pete. Goodbye."

Dana replaced the receiver, drew a steadying breath, then started across the room to answer the insistent summons at the door.

Kurt stood outside Dana's motel room and glowered at the wooden panel. The rain had finally stopped around midafternoon, but the air was damp and chilly. He'd been on his way home for the night, he was hungry, and he'd been none too pleased with himself when he realized he was heading for the Whitehorn Motel.

Dana Bailey, damn her, he fumed, had never been far from his mind and memory since he brought her to the motel yesterday morning.

When the day dawned with cold rain and a dark, gloomy sky, he'd envisioned her cooped up in the hotel room, all alone in a strange town, caught up in a situation she'd inadvertently become a major part of.

The day had no doubt seemed endless to Dana, a series of long, long hours. Depressing, lonely hours.

When he found himself driving toward the motel, he'd rationalized his actions by telling himself he had to be certain that Dana wasn't contemplating a cut-and-run.

He'd actually managed to believe that explanation for a full thirty seconds before admitting to himself that he wanted to see Dana, to be certain she wasn't totally miserable in her present circumstances.

It mattered to him, he had to be sure, that Dana Bailey wasn't crying.

Now? Kurt thought angrily, knocking on the door again. He wished he'd gone straight home. He was standing there like an idiot, chilled to the bone, starving to death, and Dana couldn't be bothered to answer the door. Her car was parked next to his vehicle. She was in there, all right, and for some reason she was ignoring his presence.

So forget it. Let her cry, brood, sulk, whatever the hell she might be doing. He really didn't give a rip if she...

The door opened, and Dana was standing there, surprise evident on her face.

"Kurt," she said. "Why are you here? Do you have news of a trial date?"

"Hello," Kurt said dryly. "How are you this evening, Detective Noble? Would you like to come inside where it's warm?"

"Oh, yes, I'm sorry."

Dana stepped back to allow Kurt to enter the room,

then closed the door behind him. He turned to face her, still frowning.

"What took you so long to answer the door?" he said. "Were you in another wing of the estate?"

"I was...I was getting dressed. It has been such a damp, chilly day that I took a long soak in a hot tub."

She's lying, Kurt thought. If Dana had been soaking in a hot bathtub, her skin would be flushed from the warmth of the water. Instead, she was very pale, appeared tired and tense.

She looked, once again, like someone who needed a comforting hug. But this time, by damn, he had enough sense not to volunteer for the job.

"Would you care to sit down?" Dana said, sweeping one hand in the direction of the chair by the table.

I need a hug, Kurt Noble, her mind yelled. The memory of being held in Kurt's strong arms was so vivid. The remembrance had never been far from her beleaguered mind, bringing with it every sensuous detail of the kisses shared with Kurt.

She hadn't been expecting to find him at her door, hadn't had time to prepare a physical and emotional defense against the effect he had on her. He seemed to be filling the small room to overflowing with his masculine magnetism, making it difficult to breathe.

"I'll stand, thanks," Kurt said. "I just stopped by to see how you're doing. It was a rather cold, dreary day, and I thought it might have been tough going."

"Where I'm going is out of my mind," Dana said, planting her hands on her jean-clad hips, "and it's not tough at all. I'm a blink away from being there."

Kurt chuckled. "Oh."

"Don't smile," she said, nearly yelling. "Don't you dare produce that damnable sexy smile. I'm going crazy staring at these four walls, Kurt Noble. Are you understanding me? I'm not going to be worth diddly as a witness at the oh-so-important trial if I'm babbling in a corner.''

"That's a good point," Kurt said, nodding. "Get your coat.''

"What?''

"I'm taking you out for some good old-fashioned cooking. We're having dinner at the Hip Hop Café.''

"Oh, well, I… Yes, all right.''

"Unless, of course, you're afraid you'll catch a cold by going outside after just having had a warm bath?''

"I'll risk it," Dana said, glaring at him.

"Mmm.''

The Hip Hop was doing a brisk business, despite the inclement weather. It was meat-loaf-and-baked-potato night at the café, a favorite blue plate special among many of the citizens of Whitehorn.

Seated in one of the booths, Dana glanced around.

"People," she said. "Living, breathing, talking, smiling people. Fantastic. Human beings. Music to my ears.''

"I hear you, Dana," Kurt said. "The circumstances you're in are not the greatest.''

If he only knew, she thought dryly.

"Look," Kurt went on, "if the weather is better tomorrow, why don't you check out the shops, stroll around town? I'm not holding you prisoner in that motel room. You're free to come and go.''

"As long as I stay in Whitehorn.''

"That can't be helped. We want the scum convicted.''

"Yes, I know,' she said, sighing. "How is the man who was shot? Clem, isn't it?"

"Yes. He's still in a coma. The doctors can't predict how it's going to go. The whole town is pulling for him. Everyone knows Clem. He taught a lot of us in elementary school."

"Now there's a sobering thought," Dana said, smiling. "I bet you were a handful when you were a little boy."

"I was a perfect angel." Kurt paused. "You have a lovely smile, Dana Bailey. Seeing you smile just now makes me realize how much time you spend frowning."

"As you said, Kurt, my present circumstances are not the greatest."

"True."

"Meat loaf, meat loaf," Janie Carson said, sliding a plate in front of each of them. "Enjoy. I have to work a double shift on meat-loaf night, so you'd better love every bite. Bye." She hurried away.

Dana picked up her fork. "Did we order meat loaf?"

"That's all that's offered tonight. I hope you like it."

Dana took a bite, chewed and swallowed. "It's delicious."

"Good," Kurt said, beginning to eat.

Dana glanced around the crowded, noisy room again.

"So," she said, "all these people came here this evening because of the meat loaf?"

"Yep."

"How charming." Dana laughed. "I mean it. It's so delightfully small-townish. I don't think that's a word, but... It's sort of like a big family sharing a meat-loaf dinner. That's nice, it really is."

"A lot different from Chicago. Right?"

"Oh, heavens, yes. The pace there is maddening, and... I never said I was from Chicago."

"You just confirmed what I suspected. It's not a big deal, is it? The fact that I know where you're from?"

"No. No, of course not. But are you ever *not* being a detective?"

"Oh, yes, ma'am," Kurt said, looking directly at her. "There are definitely times when my profession is the furthest thing from my mind."

Like when he was holding Dana, he thought, kissing Dana. *Noble, eat your meat loaf.*

Dana tore her gaze from Kurt's and concentrated on her meal.

She was ignoring the increased tempo of her heart that was the result of being in close proximity to this man, she told herself. She wasn't thinking about Kurt's lips, his taste, his aroma, the strength of his arms, the muscled power of his body. She was focusing on meat loaf.

"Here we go," Kurt said. "You think that gathering for meat loaf is small-townish? I can top that. Winona Cobbs just came in the door. She's our resident psychic, palm reader, the whole nine yards. She owns a place called Stop 'n' Swap outside of town. Everyone ends up browsing around out there eventually. Some folks believe she's nuts. I think she's great, a very classy lady." He waved. "Winona! Over here."

A short, round woman with gray hair and wearing

a multicolored dress with a swirling skirt hurried to answer Kurt's summons.

"Hello, dear," she said, giving him a peck on the cheek. "I can't join you. I'm dining with Homer Gilmore, the crazy old coot."

"Winona, I'd like you to meet Dana Bailey," Kurt said. "She's the one—"

"Who decked the perp who shot Clem," Winona finished for him, extending her hand to Dana. Dana smiled and shook Winona's offered hand. "The folks of Whitehorn are mighty grateful to you, Dana dear, for staying on so you can testify against that awful man who hurt our Clem."

"Well, I… Well…" Dana shrugged.

Winona released Dana's hand and turned to Kurt.

"Dear boy," she said, "come outside with me for one second, will you please? I couldn't get the key out of the ignition in my truck, the temperamental thing. Your meat loaf won't get cold if we hurry. It was lovely meeting you, Dana dear."

"The pleasure was mine," Dana said, smiling. "Maybe I'll come browse at your place. Kurt recommends it."

"I'll put the kettle on for tea when you arrive," Winona said. "I'd love to read your tea leaves," she added with a wink. Dana felt the color rise in her cheeks and stared down at her dinner.

Kurt slid out of the booth and followed Winona out of the Hip Hop.

"My truck is fine," Winona said, once they were standing on the sidewalk. "I wanted to speak to you alone, Kurt."

"What is it, Winona?"

"It's your Dana, dear."

Kurt frowned. "She isn't mine."

"Hush and listen. I sensed, felt… No, it's not like when I had visions of a woman with two faces, which turned out to be the fact that Mary Jo Kincaid was actually Lexine Baxter. No, what I saw regarding your Dana is different from that."

"She isn't mine. What did you see?"

"A woman with two faces, Kurt, but not layered like Mary Jo and Lexine. They were standing side by side. Two Danas. The same face. But standing next to each other."

"What in the hell does *that* mean?"

"How should *I* know, dear? *You're* the detective. Now! Let's go enjoy some Hip Hop meat loaf."

Chapter Five

For the first time since she'd fled from Chicago in the dead of night, Dana found herself actually relaxing and enjoying herself.

Kurt introduced her to what seemed like an endless stream of people who stopped by the booth to say hello. Everyone expressed gratitude for Dana's willingness to help convict the man who had shot Clem.

Her conscience was pricking her a bit, Dana realized, as she knew she was staying in Whitehorn to testify because she had been ordered to do so under the letter of the law.

But Kurt appeared comfortable in allowing her to take credit for a humanitarian act, so she basked in the warmth and friendliness being extended toward her by the folks of Whitehorn.

She even laughed aloud several times at some teasing being directed at Kurt by people who had known him since the day he was born.

It was meat-loaf night at the Hip Hop Café in Whitehorn, Montana, and Dana felt like a member of the family who had gathered to savor the delicious home-cooked meal.

"Are you ready to go?" Kurt asked finally. "There are people waiting for this booth."

"Yes, of course, but… Well, I hate to end the evening. I had a wonderful time, Kurt. Thank you for bringing me here."

"You bet," he said, sliding out of the booth.

As Kurt settled the bill, his mind once again focused on what Winona had said.

There were two Danas standing side by side? he thought. Maybe there was nothing ominous or complicated about Winona's vision. He'd seen Dana smile tonight, and laugh right out loud. She'd lost that tense, tight demeanor, and been fun to be with.

That could very well explain what Winona had sensed, seen: the uptight Dana, the relaxed and real Dana. The two faces of Dana Bailey.

Kurt frowned as he and Dana left the café and he assisted her into his vehicle. He went around to the other side, and within minutes was driving away from the café.

There was just one thing niggling at him, he knew, and it was Dana's reluctance to say where she had been going and why when she stopped at the convenience store in Whitehorn. The purchases she'd made indicated that she was not anticipating returning home anytime soon.

Dana had secrets.

Was that fact the basis of what Winona had seen?

A two-faced Dana in the negative sense? Hell, he hoped not. He was still on emotional overload from trusting and believing in the wrong woman. He had nowhere to put it if it happened again.

Dana shifted in her seat to look out the rear window of the Blazer.

"What was that building across from the café that had all the lights on?"

"The library." Kurt chuckled. "They stay open late on meat-loaf night. It cuts way down on overdue books, because so many people are coming into the Hip Hop and drop their books off on the way to dinner."

"Maybe I'll go there tomorrow. I've read the novel I got at the convenience store. Would they issue me a temporary card so I can check out books?"

Kurt pressed on the brake. "I'll take care of it right now."

Dana reached across the seat and placed her hand on Kurt's forearm.

"You don't have to give up your entire evening for me," she said.

"It's no problem," he said, turning the vehicle around. "There's no one waiting for me at home except a bunch of pesky stray cats."

"Cats?"

"While I'm here in Whitehorn, I'm staying in the house where I grew up. My mother died a few years back, but the stray cats put the word out that there is a Noble in the house again. I'm feeding them out of respect for my mother, but they're bugging the hell out of me."

"And your father? Where is he?"

Kurt shrugged. "I have no idea. He split when

Leigh and I were kids. My mother raised us the best she could. She was a fine woman." He paused. "Do your parents live in Chicago?"

Dana shook her head. "They were killed five years ago in a small plane that went down in a snowstorm in Colorado. They had gone to Aspen for a skiing weekend, and... Well, they never came back."

"That's rough," Kurt said quietly. "Do you have brothers and sisters?"

He parked in front of the library and shut off the ignition.

"I have a sister," Dana said, unfastening her seat belt. She opened the door. "We're identical twins."

Kurt's hand shot out, and he gripped Dana's arm.

"What?" he said.

Dana looked at him questioningly. "I have an identical twin sister. Well, we look exactly alike, but our personalities are as different as day and night, North Pole, South Pole, and every other example of opposites you could come up with. Natalie and I have nothing in common whatsoever."

"A twin sister," Kurt said, a smile breaking across his face. "Two Danas standing next to each other. There's nothing sinister about *that*."

"What on earth are you talking about?"

Kurt slid his hand down to clasp Dana's hand, his thumb gently stroking her fingers.

"Winona Cobbs is a psychic, remember? When I went outside with her, she told me that she'd had a vision of you with two faces. Not layered faces, like a mask, but two of you standing side by side. She thought I ought to know."

"I see," Dana said, looking at him intently. "So

you couldn't help but wonder if I was engaging in some kind of duplicity.''

"It crossed my mind."

"And now?"

"Well, you just explained it. Winona picked up on the fact that you have an identical twin. End of story." He laughed and shook his head. "I'll be damned. That Winona is something, isn't she?"

Dana managed to produce a small smile. "She certainly is."

Kurt gave Dana's hand a squeeze, then, still smiling, got out of the vehicle. As they walked toward the front entrance to the library, he looked up at the sky and commented on the fact that the clouds were moving on through, revealing a smattering of twinkling stars.

Dana said something she hoped sounded appropriate, while willing a rush of panic to dissipate.

Dear heaven, she thought frantically, she had to get out of this town. Winona Cobbs was a bona fide psychic. So, okay, Kurt was accepting the existence of Natalie as a perfectly reasonable explanation of Winona's vision of a two-faced Dana.

But what if Winona had more visions? What if she saw Dana running from police officers? Or saw her in handcuffs, or jail, or...

Calm down, Dana Bailey.

Kurt was no longer dwelling on what Winona had told him, Dana thought. For now, the danger, the crisis, had passed. Darn it, why had she mentioned the library? Every moment she spent with Kurt was one more moment when she might slip up and say the wrong thing.

Or *do* the wrong thing?

When Kurt held her hand, then stroked it in that tantalizing rhythm with his callused thumb, she'd felt the heat of desire begin to pulse low within her, in a matching tempo.

Oh, yes, indeed, Kurt Noble was dangerous. He was a threat to her not only because he was an officer of the law, but also because he was a man who was constantly evoking heated passion within her. Passion like nothing she had ever experienced before.

Forget that part, Dana ordered herself. She'd grab a couple of books from the library, plead fatigue and ask Kurt to take her back to the motel. In the meantime, the key was to keep attention away from herself and directed toward Kurt. Fine.

"Kurt," she said, as they entered the building, "you said you were staying in your childhood home *while* you were in Whitehorn. That sounds as if you're only here temporarily."

Kurt nodded. "I am. I'm on leave from the Seattle police force."

"If you're on leave, then why are you still performing in the role of a police officer? I mean, aren't leaves of absences supposed to be like vacations, or whatever?"

"It's a long story. What kind of books do you like to read?"

Dana stopped walking and turned to look directly at Kurt.

"My, my," she said, lifting her chin, "the man has secrets. But then again, maybe you're just a private person, as I am."

Kurt looked at her for a long moment.

"Maybe," he said finally. "Where is this going, Dana? Are we playing the game you-show-me-yours-and-I'll-show-you-mine? You tell me where you're headed and why, and I'll explain why I'm not in Seattle?''

''I'm not playing at any game, Detective Noble.''

''Aren't you?'' he said, narrowing his eyes.

''What on earth is your problem?''

Dana glanced around quickly, suddenly remembering that she was in a library. She glared at Kurt and lowered her voice to a near whisper when she spoke again.

''A few minutes ago,'' she said, ''you were tickled pink because you'd discovered what Winona Cobbs's vision, or whatever it was, meant. Now? You're back in your cop mode, questioning every little thing I do or say. Well, I've had enough of your mood swings. Forget the stupid books. Just take me back to the motel.''

Kurt let out a pent-up breath, puffing his cheeks in the process.

''You're right,'' he said, raising both hands. ''I humbly apologize.''

''You do?'' Dana said, surprise evident on her face.

''I certainly do, Ms. Bailey. I shall make a tremendous effort to curb my naturally suspicious nature.'' Kurt grinned. ''Do you want to check out books with words, or just pictures?''

Dana laughed and shook her head. ''You're cuckoo.''

''It helps in my line of work. Come on. Let's go to the desk and get you an official library card.''

As they started across the room, a man came out of the stacks and headed in their direction. Kurt stopped walking, and Dana halted next to him. When the man arrived in front of them, he extended his hand to Kurt.

"J.D.," Kurt said, shaking his hand.

"Kurt," J.D. said. He looked at Dana. "Ah, the heroine of the robbery fiasco. Have you ever considered playing professional baseball, Ms. Bailey? You've got a fine pitching arm there."

Dana smiled. "I hardly remember throwing that soda can. You're the man who came into the store behind Kurt, aren't you? The one who helped Clem?"

"Yes, ma'am. J. D. Cade, at your service."

What was this? Kurt thought crossly. Dana and J.D. were smiling at each other like two people in a toothpaste commercial. Just turning on the charm. Oozing politeness. Well, enough of this malarkey.

"What brings you into town, J.D.?" Kurt said.

"A couple of things," J.D. said, directing his attention to Kurt again. "One is Hip Hop meat loaf. I like to wait until it's not so crowded over there, so I was doing the second thing on my list."

"Oh, yeah?" Kurt said.

"I was researching Native American ceremonies, symbols, what have you. I thought I might discover what message was being delivered by those chickens I found on the fence. I'm not saying it was someone from the res who did it, but it could have been made to appear that it was."

"Good thinking," Kurt said. "Judd told me about the chickens. Did you find anything in here that would give us a clue as to what those birds meant?"

"Nope." J.D. shook his head. "Not a thing."

"Chickens?" Dana said.

"Dead chickens were hung on a fence out at the Kincaid ranch," J.D. said. "It's just one more in a long list of weird doings out there. Rumors are running wild that the ranch is haunted by ghosts. We had another hand quit today because of the chickens. Someone is really stirring up a lot of trouble.''

''For heaven's sake,'' Dana said, ''why? Does this Kincaid person who owns the ranch have enemies who would do these types of things?''

''No, and that only adds to the mystery of why this is being done,'' J.D. said. ''The owner is a three-year-old sweetheart named Jennifer. The spread is held in trust for her by her adoptive father, Sterling McCallum.''

''This doesn't make any sense,'' Dana said.

''Tell me about it,'' Kurt said. ''Try being on the police force that's attempting to get to the bottom of it. Judd was fuming about those chickens. The sheriff is very angry and very frustrated.''

''So are those of us on the ranch.'' J.D. frowned. ''What's left of us, that is. We're constantly short-handed because the drifters coming through who we hire get scared off by the stuff that's happening.'' He paused. ''Well, I'd best be on my way, or there won't be any meat loaf left for dinner.''

''It was delicious,'' Dana said.

''Good evening to you,'' J.D. said, touching the tips of his fingers to the edge of his Stetson. ''Kurt,'' he added with a nod.

''Good night,'' Dana said.

''See ya, J.D.,'' Kurt said.

Dana turned slightly and watched until J.D. had gone out the door of the library. When she looked at Kurt again, he was glowering.

''*Now* what is the matter?'' she said.

"I was just wondering if you got enough of an eyeful of J. D. Cade's butt."

"I was not looking at his...his posterior. But if I had been, what business would it be of yours? I'm perfectly free to scrutinize anyone's butt, to crudely quote you, that I darn well please. If it wasn't so ridiculous, I'd say you sound jealous."

Dana marched off in the direction of the counter.

"The very idea," she muttered. "Absolutely ridiculous."

No joke, Kurt thought, following Dana at a much slower pace. *Ridiculous* didn't even begin to describe his behavior. But he'd felt it, all right, the bite from the green-eyed monster, when Dana and J.D. were doing their toothpaste-commercial routine, then again when Dana stared at J.D. while he was leaving the library.

What was the matter with him? Kurt fumed. Dana wasn't his lady, his woman, or any other possessive label that he might come up with.

No, she wasn't his, nor would he want her to be. She was just passing through town, a blip on the screen, a here-today-gone-tomorrow person.

And she still refused to tell him where she was going and why.

He didn't need a woman in his life who had secrets. He didn't need or want *any* woman muddling up his existence again. He'd learned his lesson the hard way, and he was steering clear of that arena, thank you very much.

So what if he was continually reliving the kisses he'd shared with Dana, the feel of her luscious body nestled against him? It didn't mean a thing, other than that he was a normal, healthy man.

It was perfectly understandable that Dana Bailey was turning him inside out, causing hot, coiled desire to throb low in his body when he was close to her. She was a lovely woman, who was intelligent, feisty and fun and evoked emotions in him of protectiveness and...well, yeah, possessiveness.

But that made sense, because Dana was caught up in the mess that had taken place at the convenience store. She was all alone in a strange town, cooped up in a dreary motel room. There were times when she appeared so tired, so tense, so vulnerable.

When he least expected it, Dana looked like someone who needed a hug.

No doubt about it, Kurt thought, shaking his head. Dana was driving him out of his ever-lovin' mind. He would definitely be as relieved as she would be when the trial was over and she would leave Whitehorn.

Just go. Disappear. Forever. Good. Right?

Kurt reached the desk and Dana turned to smile at him.

"I have a library card," she said. "I'm officially official. Come on, Kurt, you can help me pick out some yummy books. This is going to be fun."

Kurt smiled in spite of himself as they went into the stacks where fiction was shelved.

Yes, sir, he thought, Dana was definitely driving him crazy.

Jessica Larson McCallum entered the large living room where her husband, Sterling, sat talking with their attorney, Wendell Hargrove.

In his early sixties, Wendell was still an extremely handsome man. Tall and trim, he had thick, wavy white hair. His demeanor was always dignified and stately, resulting in an unspoken demand for respect, which he invariably received. There were rumors in the wind that Wendell was going to run for office. Other gossips insisted he would soon be appointed a judge.

Sterling stopped speaking as Jessica crossed the room. He extended his hand to her, and she sat down next to him on the sofa, with their fingers entwined.

"Is Jennifer asleep?" Sterling said.

Jessica frowned. "Yes, she didn't even stay awake long enough to hear the end of the story I was reading to her. She usually tries to con me into reading a second story. I hope she isn't coming down with something."

"She's a busy bee," Sterling said, chuckling. "She probably just wore herself out today."

"I remember when my three daughters were small," Wendell said. "They were bundles of energy, but little ones seem to know when they need to wind down and get some catch-up rest. I wouldn't be concerned about Jennifer falling asleep earlier than usual, Jessica."

"I'm sure you're right, Wendell," Jessica said. "She'll probably pop up at dawn tomorrow, ready to play. I hope to see rosy cheeks in the morning, too. She was awfully pale tonight." She paused. "Well, I've certainly interrupted whatever you gentlemen were discussing."

"You're a lovely distraction from the subject matter, my dear," Wendell said.

"I'll second that," Sterling said, giving Jessica's hand a loving squeeze.

"Unfortunately," Wendell said, "there has been another incident at the ranch, Jessica. That new hand,

J. D. Cade, found dead chickens tied to a fence in very odd but exacting order.''

"Oh, dear," Jessica said, sighing. "Who is doing this, and why? I just don't understand what someone hopes to gain by causing such unrest at the ranch. Rand Harding is having a difficult time keeping men on the payroll because of these bizarre happenings."

"That's sadly true," Wendell said. "Another hand was frightened off today. He said he wasn't working on a spread that was haunted."

"Judd Hensley still doesn't have a clue as to who is behind this," Sterling said.

"No, he doesn't." Wendell shook his head. "Sterling, I've given this situation a great deal of thought. As your attorney, I'm advising you to close down the ranch until we can get to the bottom of this trouble. As it presently stands, the operation is becoming a financial drain, which isn't in Jennifer's best interests."

Sterling released Jessica's hand and got to his feet. He crossed the room and stared into the leaping flames of the fire in the huge fireplace. Several long, silent minutes passed, and then he turned to look at Wendell.

"No," Sterling said. "That's probably what whoever is behind this wants me to do. No, Wendell, I won't knuckle under to this nonsense. The ranch will continue to operate, business as usual."

"I truly believe you're making a mistake, Sterling," Wendell said.

"I appreciate your concern," Sterling said, "but my mind is made up."

"And that, as they say," Jessica said, smiling, "is

that. You ought to recognize that stubborn set to Sterling's jaw that indicates that a subject is closed, Wendell. So! Who is ready for some homemade apple pie?''

Chapter Six

The next afternoon, Judd Hensley called Kurt into the sheriff's office and informed him that he should pack a suitcase and head for Billings.

"You'll be representing our department at the trial of those two guys who were pulling the roofing scam," Judd said. "The prosecution is bringing in cops from quite a few towns where people were ripped off. Here's a file with the statements, photographs, what have you, that you'll present as evidence."

"How long will I be stuck down there?" Kurt said, frowning. "Even more, why me? I wasn't even in Whitehorn when those yo-yos came through."

"No telling when they'll call you to testify. They want you to be in court every day, though, so you'll be available. As for why you?" Judd smiled. "Because you're low man on the totem pole around here, the last one to go on the payroll. This assignment is boredom in its purest form. I'm sure not going to get a volunteer for the job.''

"Cripe," Kurt said, accepting the file. He paused, then snapped his fingers. "I can't go, Judd. I'm responsible for feeding a whole slew of cats at my place. Think about it. They'll be starving, crying for food, hungry and confused because I deserted them. I have to stay in Whitehorn to care for those poor homeless animals.''

Judd chuckled. "Nice try, Noble, but put a cork in it. You're wasting your breath.''

"Hell. I suppose I have to wear a tie in the courtroom, too.''

"Yep.''

"You have no heart, Hensley," Kurt said. "You're like that character in *The Wizard of Oz*. No heart.''

"Goodbye, Kurt.''

"Cripe.''

Ten minutes later, Kurt was driving toward the Whitehorn Motel.

He'd recruit Dana, he decided, to feed the dumb cats. Heaven knew she had plenty of free time on her hands. She could break up her day of having her nose poked in a book by driving out to his place and tending to the furry moochers on his porch.

Books, he thought. The library. Last night. For some strange reason, helping Dana choose a selection of novels *had* been fun, just as she'd said it would be.

He and Dana had laughed so loud at one point, when she delivered a dramatic reading of the back blurb on a book, he was certain they were going to be tossed right out of the building.

Dana had ended up with six books in a wide variety of reading material. She had everything from mysteries to historical romances to a biography of Eleanor Roosevelt. Interesting choices. But then, Dana Bailey was a very interesting woman.

Their lighthearted mood had prevailed while he drove her back to the motel, Kurt mused. Then, before he knew what hit him, Dana had thanked him for a lovely evening, zipped into her room and left him standing outside, staring at the door like an imbecile.

Well, what had he expected her to do? he asked himself. Invite him in for a nightcap? Dana had been very smart to leave him on the sidewalk. The attraction between them, the sensual pull, the simmering desire, was always there, just below the surface. The two of them alone in a room where the main piece of furniture was a bed was dangerous, just asking for trouble.

Yes, Dana had done the right thing by rushing into the room…alone. Her actions, however, had changed his up mood into a downer, causing him to grumble under his breath all the way home.

Lord, that didn't make sense. He didn't want any part of the emotional complications that would arise if he and Dana made love. He would have refused an invitation to enter her room last night, even if she'd issued one.

He had a sneaky suspicion that he'd been grumpy as a bear because Dana had called the shots instead of him, even though she'd done exactly the right thing. Macho crap sure was a pain in the butt at times.

Kurt parked next to Dana's car in the motel lot,

and moments later knocked on her door. She answered the summons quickly, with a book in one hand.

"Hello, Kurt," she said, smiling. "You're a nice surprise. Come in."

Come in? Kurt thought. Last night she'd closed the door in his face. Today he was being invited in. Female rationale was a pain in the butt at times, too.

Kurt entered the room, and Dana closed the door behind him.

"Do you have news of a trial date?" Dana said.

"Yes, but not the trial you're concerned about," he said. "Judd will contact you if there's information you should know. The public defender is dragging his feet a bit, with the hope that Clem will come out of the coma and it's apparent that he'll recover."

"Can he delay for something like that?"

"Not for long, but Clem's condition will have a tremendous impact on the sentence the perp will get."

"Yes, I suppose it would." Dana sighed. "So here I sit."

"Well," Kurt said, smiling, "at least you've got a stack of books to read. There are a lot of people who would be envious of the fact that you can spend your days curled up with a good book."

"It gets very old, very fast."

"Yes," Kurt said, nodding, "I'm sure it does." He paused. "Dana, I have a favor to ask of you. Do you remember my telling you about the cats who hang around at my place?"

"Yes. Hearing you talk about them made me miss Lucy and Ethel."

"Who?"

"My two. They're spoiled rotten, and I adore them.

My friend Todd is feeding them, but I doubt if he's staying around to play with them, poor babies."

My *friend* Todd? Kurt mentally repeated. How good a friend, what kind of a friend, was her buddy Todd? *Damn it, Noble, forget it.* He really didn't care one way or another about some jerk named Todd who was Dana's *friend.* Todd. What a wimpy name. The guy probably had his nails manicured once a week.

"Kurt?" Dana said. "You were saying something about a favor?"

"Oh, yeah. Listen, I have to go to Billings to testify at a trial. I'm not certain how long I'll be gone. I'm stuck there until they call me to the witness stand."

"Do tell," Dana said dryly. "Well, it certainly serves you right, considering that's exactly what you're doing to me."

"I figured you'd get in your licks on that one. So, okay, we're even. Tit for tat. I was wondering if you'd feed the cats at my place while I'm gone?"

"Oh. Well, sure, I could do that."

"I'll draw you a map of how to get to the house, although it's a straight shot out of town. There's a bunch of cat food in the kitchen. Feed the beasts once a day on the front porch. Don't let even one of them sneak inside the house."

"Yes, sir."

"Hey, I really appreciate this."

"No problem. I'll need a key to your house."

"The door isn't locked. It never has been, for as long as I can remember."

"Doesn't that go against your training as a police officer?"

"I was a resident of Whitehorn for more years than I've been a cop."

Dana nodded. "That makes sense, I guess." She paused. "I'm looking forward to tending to the cats. It will make me feel productive for a while each day. Thank you for... well, for trusting me to roam around in your home, Kurt." She looked directly into his eyes. "You do, don't you? Trust me?"

Dana Bailey didn't play fair, Kurt thought. Those enormous blue eyes of hers could melt ice on the coldest Montana day.

He knew he had niggling doubts about Dana because of her reluctance to explain why she was on the road, where she was going. Warning bells went off in his head whenever she skittered around answering questions about the purpose and destination of her off-the-main-route trip.

But when he was this close to her, gazing into those incredible eyes, the doubts were overshadowed by a haze of desire that instantly consumed him.

"Yes," Kurt heard himself say, "I do trust you, Dana Bailey."

"Thank you," she whispered. "That means a great deal to me right now, because... Well, it just does."

Kurt frowned slightly.

His trust in her meant a great deal *right now?* his mind echoed. Because...because why? What was Dana trying to tell him? Were there people who *didn't* trust her *right now?* Was she in some kind of trouble? Lord, was she in some sort of danger?

He'd been concentrating on the question of where Dana was going. Should he have been focused on the possibility that she was running *away* from someone in Chicago?

Kurt framed Dana's face in his hands.

"Listen to me," he said. "Trust works both ways. You can trust me, Dana, you really can. Talk to me."

Oh, she wanted to, Dana thought. She wanted to be wrapped in the safe, comforting cocoon of Kurt's embrace, to feel his strong arms acting as a barrier between her and the world beyond.

She wanted to pour out her heart to him, tell him about the living nightmare she was existing in, plead with him to help her prove her innocence by finding Natalie.

She wanted to rest her weary head on the solid wall of Kurt Noble's chest and weep until the tears of fear, betrayal and loneliness were no more.

But she couldn't, just couldn't. Kurt was an officer of the law first, a man second. She had to remember that. *She had to.*

"I'll take good care of the cats," she said, her voice trembling.

"Ah, Dana..." Kurt said, shaking his head. "What's going on? Whatever it is, you don't have to square off against it all alone. I'm here. Do you realize that? I *am* here for you."

"Kurt, don't," she said. "Please don't. You're going to make me cry, and if I start I won't be able to stop. I can't...I can't *talk to you,* not now, not yet."

Kurt studied her face for a long moment, his heart thundering.

Dana *was* in trouble, his mind hammered. And in danger? Damn, he wanted to fix it all for her, whatever it was, slay the dragons, make her smile again and hear her laugh right out loud.

But he couldn't do any of those things if she continued to shut him out, keep him on the other side of her wall of silence. He felt so helpless, so frustrated.

"Damn," Kurt said, then lowered his head and captured Dana's mouth in a rough, searing kiss.

Dana fought against threatening tears, then gave way to the desire suffusing her, allowing it to push aside everything except the want, the need, to make love with Kurt. The book in her hand dropped unheeded to the floor, and her arms floated upward to encircle his neck.

She returned the kiss in total abandon, drinking in the taste, the aroma, the protective strength, of Kurt. The nightmare was replaced by passion, and she welcomed it, rejoiced in it and the heat it brought to the chill of fear within her.

The kiss gentled, and passions soared.

A groan of need rumbled deep in Kurt's chest, and Dana gloried in the masculine sound, knowing Kurt wanted her as much as she did him.

They were not in a shabby motel room in Whitehorn, Montana, she thought dreamily. They were in a beautiful field of fragrant wildflowers that would be a bed created by nature just for them. They would make love beneath a crystal-clear blue sky, their bodies warmed by a golden sun. It would be their private world, where no one else was granted entry.

Kurt raised his head and drew a ragged breath.

"Dana, I..." he began, his voice gritty.

"Want you," she said. "Yes. Yes, and I want you. Here, in the midst of the wildflowers, we'll make exquisite love together."

"What?"

"Make love with me, Kurt. Please."

No! Kurt's mind yelled. Dana had secrets, was keeping things from him, wasn't being totally open and honest with him. He'd vowed to never again be rendered vulnerable by a woman who was not who she appeared to be. He mustn't do this. No, he would not, could not, make love with Dana Bailey. But...

"Kurt? Please?"

But right now he didn't give a damn about Dana's secrets, he told himself, about what he didn't know about her.

"Yes," he said, "we'll make love. Here. In the wildflowers."

They moved to the side of the bed, then shed their clothes as quickly as possible, fingers fumbling with stubborn buttons. When they stood naked before each other, Dana's breath caught as she saw the vivid, angry scar on Kurt's shoulder.

"What happened?" she said, searching his face with a troubled gaze.

"It's old news."

"No, it's not old news. That scar is from a recent wound. It's still healing."

"Shh," he said, and then his mouth melted over hers.

They tumbled onto the bed, Kurt automatically catching his weight on his uninjured side. Their need was earthy, raw and urgent. They touched, explored, discovered, hands, lips, tongues, never still, savoring all.

Their breathing was labored, echoing in the quiet room. Hearts beat in racing tempos. With an unspoken agreement that they could wait no longer, they meshed, Kurt surging deep within Dana's moist femininity, bringing to her all that he was as a man.

The rhythm they set was thundering, pounding, carrying them up and away from the flowers to fly through the blue heaven above. Higher. Hotter. Wild and wonderful. Ecstasy.

"Kurt!"

Dana clung to him as she was flung into oblivion. He followed her in the next moment to where she had gone, calling her name in a voice not recognizable to him as his own.

He collapsed against her, spent, ignoring the pain radiating through his shoulder and down his arm.

They were still, sated, savoring, as hearts slowed and breathing returned to normal levels.

"Oh, my," Dana whispered.

"I'm crushing you," Kurt said, then moved off her to lie by her side.

"That was..." Dana said, then words failed her.

"Yes, it was," Kurt said. "Unbelievable."

"And wrong, I suppose," she said, with a sigh.

"Not if we agree that it wasn't. It was ours, Dana. We both wanted this to happen."

"Yes, you're right. It was ours. A memory to cherish. And I will." Dana paused. "But, Kurt? I hope you don't think that I make a habit of... What I mean is, I hardly know you, but... Oh, drat, I'm starting to babble."

"I understand what you're saying," he said quietly, sifting his fingers through her tousled hair. "Will I still respect you in the morning? Yes, Dana Bailey, I most definitely will."

"Thank you. I feel like Alice in Wonderland after she zoomed down the rabbit's hole. Nothing in my life is how it was. What just happened between us is out of character for me, too, but I refuse to regret that we made love."

"Good. That's good." He brushed a strand of hair

off her cheek with his fingertips. "You feel like Alice because of what you witnessed at the convenience store, and the fact that you have to stay on here in Whitehorn?"

"I...um... Yes, of course. Things are topsy-turvy, in my once well-ordered existence. Well-ordered. Now that I think about it, that means borderline boring at times." Dana laughed softly. "My life at the moment is definitely *not* boring. It's unreal, crazy, bizarre and... Oh well, never mind."

Kurt frowned. "Those are pretty heavy-duty adjectives for someone whose day consists of sitting in a dinky motel room reading a book."

"I do have a life beyond Whitehorn, Montana, Kurt."

"Yes, I know you do, and you're very secretive about it."

"No more than you are about why you're in Whitehorn, instead of Seattle."

"I told you that I'm on a leave of absence from the Seattle police force."

"But you're working for Sheriff Hensley. That's not a normal leave of absence."

Kurt moved off the bed and began to dress. Dana slipped beneath the bedspread to cover her nakedness, pushing the pillow upward so that she could lean against the wall.

"It's not a major mystery," Kurt said, reaching for his shirt. "I was shot while on an undercover assignment. The doctor released me to return to desk duty, and I said I'd pass. I can work for Judd while my shoulder finishes healing. That's it. End of story. Your turn, Ms. Bailey. Where are you going and why?"

Oh, dear, Dana thought. She didn't want to lie to

Kurt, she really didn't. They'd just made exquisitely beautiful love, shared the most intimate act possible between man and woman. She cared for Kurt with emotions that went beyond physical desire. She certainly wasn't falling in love with the man—she had more sense than that—but she really did care.

"I...I'm trying to find my twin sister, Natalie," she said.

Kurt sat down on the edge of the bed and looked at Dana intently.

"Your sister is missing?" he said.

"Yes, she is," Dana said. And that was definitely the truth. If Natalie could be found, then the nightmare could end. She could prove her innocence, return to Chicago, to the career that was the focus of her existence. "I have to locate her, talk to her."

"I see," Kurt said slowly. "Are the police in Chicago helping you?"

"I've hired a private detective."

Kurt raked one hand through his hair. "Dana, excuse me if I'm overstepping here, but you and Natalie are...what? Twenty-six? Twenty-seven?"

"Twenty-eight."

"So, okay, we're not talking about a missing teenager who could be in trouble somewhere. Natalie is a grown woman, who has the right to go where she wants to." Kurt paused. "Or am I missing something here?"

Brilliant, Dana, she thought dryly. She should have known better than to think she could dish up a few crumbs of information for *Detective* Noble and have him be satisfied with the offered serving.

Oh, why did Kurt have to press, push her for more details? It really was so important to her that she not come right out and lie to him. She just didn't want to do that.

"Natalie is very headstrong," she said. "She *does* get herself into situations where she doesn't belong. She has created a nightmare of a mess, not just for herself, but for others, as well, and it's imperative that I find her so things can be set to rights."

"So why are you in Whitehorn, Montana? Has Natalie headed this way before?"

"Kurt, please," Dana said, covering one of his hands with one of hers. "I feel as though I'm under a bare lightbulb, being interrogated. I'm attempting to locate my twin sister. Can't we just leave it at that?"

No! Kurt's mind yelled. Because there was still too much that Dana wasn't telling him. His investigative instincts told him that she was skittering around the edges of the whole story, the complete truth.

Natalie had created a nightmare of a mess? For others, as well as herself? Had Natalie done something to place Dana in danger?

"Yeah, I'll let it go," he said, getting to his feet again.

Thank goodness, Dana thought.

"For now," he finished.

Dana sighed and shook her head, weary defeat sweeping over her like an oppressively heavy blanket. After making certain her bare breasts were covered with the spread, she rested her head against the wall and closed her eyes.

Kurt hunkered down to tie his shoes, his glance falling on Dana as he straightened again.

Lord, she was beautiful, he thought. Making love with Dana Bailey had been emotionally moving, had been much, much more than just physical release and satisfaction.

And now? There she sat, looking pale and vulnerable again, because he had jabbed at her, pushed and prodded for answers he felt he deserved to have.

Deserved to have? Who in the hell did he think he was? He hadn't been questioning Dana as a cop. No, it had been Kurt Noble, the man, who wanted to know her innermost secrets.

Because he'd been so out of line, Dana once again appeared tense, tired, and in need of a hug. Had he overshadowed their lovemaking, ruined her memories of what they'd shared, with his arrogant demands? Lord, he hoped not. For some reason he couldn't begin to fathom, he wanted, *needed*, Dana to treasure, as he was treasuring what had transpired between them.

Kurt dragged both hands down his face.

She was doing it again, he thought. Dana was driving him nuts. His emotions, his thoughts, his reasoning, were bouncing back and forth like Ping-Pong balls.

He trusted Dana. He doubted her. She was strong and independent. She was soft and vulnerable. She was open and honest. She was secretive and hiding things.

Ping...pong...

Dana was vibrantly alive, with a smile like sunshine, laughter like wind chimes. She was tense, closed, drawn and tired.

She was as free and uninhibited as a soaring bird when making love. She was carefully guarded by a high wall around her inner truths.

Ping...pong...

He wanted to put many, many miles between them. He wanted to pull her close and never let her go.

He wished she'd never come to Whitehorn, Montana. He now had the answer to the haunting question of what had been missing from his life.

No! No way. He wasn't getting seriously involved with a woman again. Especially one who was keeping truths from him. But Dana had become very important to him, very quickly, and...

Ping...pong...

"Damn it," Kurt said.

Dana's eyes popped open at Kurt's sudden outburst, then widened as he strode to the bed and planted his hands on either side of her hips. He leaned forward to speak close to her lips, his blue eyes blazing.

"Listen up, Ms. Bailey," he said. "I'm leaving now, going home to pack, then heading out to Billings. I don't know when I'll be back, but when I *do* return, you and I are going to have a long talk."

"But..."

"Why?" Kurt went on as though Dana hadn't spoken. "Because you're keeping things from me, no doubt about it. I've got this knot in my gut that says you might be in some kind of danger. I can't handle that, Dana. I can't deal with the thought of anything happening to you. Are you getting this?"

"Yes, but..."

"Good. That's good."

Kurt captured Dana's lips in a kiss so searing it literally stole the breath from her body. When he finally broke the kiss, he straightened and looked directly into her eyes, his own eyes radiating raw desire.

He spun on his heel, crossed to the door, yanked it

open, then slammed it closed behind him with a vibrating thud.

Dana blinked, drew a much-needed breath, then pressed trembling fingertips to her tingling lips.

Kurt Noble cared, her heart and mind hummed. At that moment, that tick of glorious time, she didn't care about the right or wrong, the wisdom or foolishness, of having her life intertwining with a police officer.

All she knew was that she cared about Kurt, and he returned that caring in kind.

All she knew was that for the first time since the nightmare created by Natalie had begun, she was suffused with warmth, instead of the chill of fear and loneliness.

Chapter Seven

She missed Kurt.

Dana sat on the front steps of the Noble home as the cats, now numbering sixteen, ate their lunch.

During the two weeks Kurt had been gone, Dana had established a routine that was becoming increasingly enjoyable, staying at Kurt's house a little longer each day.

Dana's gaze swept over the brilliant blue sky, which was dotted with pillows of white clouds. Taking a deep breath, she marveled yet again at how crisp and clear the air was, with no hint of pollution.

The blessed silence was heavenly, she mused. The few sounds that reached her were soothing; the cats munching eagerly on their room-service meal, the buzzing of a bee, the chirping of a bird.

May in Montana was marvelous, she thought, then

laughed softly, deciding she should give that slogan to the chamber of commerce.

It was so very different here from the way it was in Chicago. And *she* was different, changed, as well. In the past two weeks, she'd learned to shut off her mind when she drove into Kurt's driveway, absolutely refusing to think about Natalie and the nightmare her twin sister had created.

She could actually relax here, just be. Kurt's house was her haven, the place where she came for a sense of peace, well-being, an escape from fear of what the future held for her.

At Kurt's, she also allowed herself the luxury of taking the memories of him from the treasure chest in her heart and savoring each, one by one, every minute, every special detail.

She missed Kurt.

She wanted to see him, to drink in the sight of his tall, strong body, his dark hair sprinkled with gray, those eyes that matched the color of the Montana sky in May.

She wanted to trace Kurt's rugged features with her fingertips, then her lips, etching them indelibly in her mind.

She wanted to hear the rich masculine chuckle that rumbled in Kurt's broad chest, then match his smile with one of her own.

She wanted to fill her senses with his aroma of fresh air, soap and man.

And she wanted to make love with Kurt Noble.

One of the cats finished eating and wandered over to where Dana sat, meowing and leaning against her.

''Hello, Mama Kitty,'' Dana said, stroking the cat's

swollen stomach. ''Those babies must be due to arrive very soon. You look big enough to pop.''

The cat stretched out on the porch, then began to clean her paws as she stayed close to Dana's side. Dana watched in fascination as the unborn kittens moved within the mother-to-be, rolling, bunching, shifting.

''The miracle of birth,'' Dana said, unaware that one of her hands had floated upward to splay on her own flat stomach.

A baby, she mused. What would it feel like to have a baby growing within her, being nurtured by her body, waiting for the moment to be born?

A baby, created by the beautiful act of making love with the man of her heart. A child, who would be a unique combination of herself and that man, a human being who hadn't been here before.

A baby.

Kurt's baby.

Dana stiffened, startled by where her wandering, whimsical thoughts had taken her.

For heaven's sake, what an absurd idea, she admonished herself. Well, it was understandable, in a way. She *was* spending a great deal of time at Kurt's home, and was admittedly also spending a great deal of time thinking about Detective Noble.

The lovemaking she shared with Kurt had been like none before; so beautiful, so intense, combining the physical with the emotional in a new and wondrous way.

Oh, yes, she cared for and about Kurt. But he was part of her life as it now stood, a player in the scenario that had unfolded after she fled from Chicago in the dead of night.

Natalie would be found. The truth would be told. Dana's innocence would be determined, and her existence would return to normal, to what it had been before the nightmare had begun.

She would never see Kurt Noble again.

Dana jumped to her feet as she felt a chill sweep through her. Mama Kitty raised her head to see what the sudden commotion was, then settled again in her puddle of sunlight. Dana took a deep breath, let it out slowly, then lifted her chin.

I hereby decree, she thought, *that nothing will be thought, said or done to disturb the peace and tranquillity of these daily visits to Kurt's home. So there.*

"Okay." She turned toward the cats and clapped her hands. "Who wants to go for a walk today?"

Dana started off, having discovered over the days that there was no pattern to the independent felines' behavior. On some days, they bounded off the porch to accompany her on the trek. Other times, one or two would join her, or she might find herself walking alone.

Today, three of the cats ambled behind her, not appearing especially enthused about the exercise.

Kurt's house was surrounded by very lush country, with sloping hills, green grass, wildflowers, tall pine trees and Douglas firs.

The house itself, Dana had decided early on, could be transformed into an enchanting cottage if given a bit of tender loving care. She'd mentally painted, patched, scrubbed and rubbed, her imagination seeing the picture-perfect fruits of her labor.

In actuality, she'd hardly touched a thing inside the house, except for the huge bag of cat food. Kurt would return to find a layer of dust on top of the layer of dust, as she didn't feel comfortable stepping in and sprucing things up without having permission. So be it.

She'd been lucky to locate the house at all, Dana thought as she strolled along. Kurt had left the motel room that day without giving her the promised map.

Not wishing to become chummy with a sheriff, for heaven's sake, Dana had telephoned Kimberly at the police station to ask directions to Kurt's house.

Kimberly had laughed.

"You got stuck feeding those cats?" she'd said. "Kurt tried to wheedle out of going to Billings by telling Judd the critters would starve if he left town. Judd didn't buy it for a second."

"I would hope not," Dana had said, smiling. "Do you like cats?"

"Oh, yes. I have two of my own."

"It's a good thing you think they're nifty. I guess there's a zillion of 'em at the Noble place because Kurt's mother was always feeding the strays. She was a nice lady. Have you met Kurt's sister, Leigh, yet?"

"No. No, I haven't."

"She's really nice, too. Well, it was good talking to you, Dana, but I've got to get my filing done."

"Kimberly!"

"Hmm?"

"The directions to Kurt's house?"

"Oh, yeah," Kim had said, laughing, "that's why you called, isn't it? Okay, all you have to do is drive straight through town, and…"

And here she was, Dana thought, just as she'd been every day for the past two weeks.

And here she was…missing Kurt.

She hadn't heard a word from him, but hadn't expected to. Kurt didn't strike her as the type who would indulge in idle chitchat on the telephone. Besides, he'd made it very clear that they were going to have a heart-to-heart talk about *everything* when he returned. He'd definitely want to tackle that in person, and it was a session she was not looking forward to.

Dana sighed and told her mind to turn off, go blank, so that she could enjoy the tranquillity of her surroundings. But today her brain refused to obey the daily command.

The night before, Dana had spoken with Pete Parker, the private detective she'd hired, and his update hadn't been good. He had made absolutely no progress whatsoever in locating Natalie.

"I just don't believe this," Dana had moaned, sinking onto the edge of the bed in the motel room. "Where can she be?"

"I'll find her," Pete had said. "It's just taking longer than I figured."

And was using up her savings at a rapid pace, Dana had thought miserably.

"Do you want the rest of the bad news?" Pete had asked.

"Oh, sure, why not?" Dana had said, flipping one hand in the air.

"I talked to your pal Todd," Pete said.

"And?"

"You know those security cameras your firm had just installed to come on at night?"

"Yes. They weren't working properly, and the security outfit was supposed to come back and figure out what was wrong."

"Right," Pete had said. "Well, they finally showed

up. Are you ready for this? One of the cameras actually worked. The one in your office.

"Dana, they have a videotape of Natalie, who they believe is you, in the office after-hours on the night in question. She printed out some material from the computer, put it in an envelope, then ducked out."

"Dear heaven," Dana had whispered.

"Todd saw the film," Pete had gone on. "He said the woman looks exactly like you, is even wearing a dress he recognized as being one you'd worn to work in the past."

"Oh, Pete, this is terrible."

"Hey, I know it sounds bad, but once I find Natalie and she spills the beans, it will all be cleared up."

"But what if you never find her? This is a big world we live in, you know."

"Remember what I told you. Everyone is somewhere. I'll track her down."

"You have to. You just have to."

Dana reached the top of an incline and stopped, wrapping her hands around her elbows in a protective gesture. She swept her gaze over the majestic view before her.

Where are you, Natalie? she thought. They had never been close, had not managed to connect on any level since being little girls playing dolls together. They were simply two people who happened to have the same parents and who had grown up under the same roof.

But it still hurt, Dana thought, knowing that her twin sister had done this to her. Natalie had no conscience, no qualms at all about Dana going to jail for what she had done.

Dana shook her head, then turned and started back

to Kurt's house, the cats remaining behind to snooze in the warm, fragrant grass.

Kurt stood in the front yard of his house and watched Dana approaching slowly in the distance. A sense of anticipation swept through him, along with a flash of heated desire, as he waited for Dana to draw near.

There he stood, Kurt thought, in front of his house…such as it was…waiting for the woman who had occupied his thoughts during the day and his dreams at night through the entire two long weeks he'd been in Billings.

He was going to give himself this moment, he decided. Like an adolescent with unobtainable daydreams, he was actually going to pretend that he was an ordinary businessman who had been away on a trip and was now home.

He was going to pretend that his wife was walking toward him, having not yet realized he was there.

Behind her were two little kids, who would scamper into view at any second. His children. His and Dana's children, who had been created by lovemaking that defied description of its exquisite beauty.

He wasn't a man alone. He had a family. They were his purpose, his focus, made everything important and worthwhile. What had been missing from his life was now his, because of Dana and…

"Cripe, Noble," Kurt said aloud, "knock it off."

What in the hell was he doing? He was a realist, not a dreamer. He didn't indulge in fantasies and make-believe. He played the hand that had been dealt to him and made the best of it. End of story.

But there was Dana Bailey, coming closer and closer with each step she took.

Every attempt he made to push Dana from his mind while he was in Billings had failed miserably. She'd taken up residence in his brain and refused to budge.

In his mental vision, he'd seen her smile, heard her wind-chime laughter, watched her shift to tense and tired, guarding her secrets.

He'd seen her big blue eyes become a smoky gray with desire as she reached out her arms to receive him into her soft, womanly embrace.

He'd seen her fair cheeks flush with the heat of passion, heard her whimper in sensual need, then purr in feminine pleasure when he entered her welcoming body.

Dana.

Somehow, Kurt thought, he had to get this maddening woman out of his system, regain control of his body and emotions. She was pushing his buttons, turning him inside out, and he'd had enough.

When Dana finally spotted him, saw that he was back from Billings, he'd greet her coolly, pleasantly, then thank her for tending to the cats. That would be that.

He was, as of that very moment, canceling the proposed long talk that he'd said he and Dana were going to have. He was no longer interested in her secrets, whatever it was she was keeping from him. It was none of his business, nor did he care, who or what she was running to or from.

Kurt crossed his arms over his chest, set his jaw in a tight, hard line, and waited.

Dana glanced up, gasped softly in surprise, then stumbled slightly before continuing on her way.

Kurt, her mind hummed. Kurt was home. Her heart…goodness, her heart was suddenly beating so fast she could hear the wild tempo echoing in her ears.

Kurt was home, standing there watching her approach, looking so tall and strong, so solid and real. He was in the yard of the house she'd mentally made into a home, *their* home, cozy and clean, ready to wrap itself around them like a comforting blanket when they closed the door and shut out the world.

Oh, yes, Kurt was home.

Dana quickened her step, then threw caution to the wind and began to run…to Kurt.

Before he realized he had moved, Kurt opened his arms as Dana ran into his embrace. He pulled her close, ignoring the pain in his shoulder from the impact of her delectable body slamming against him. She flung her arms around his neck as he lowered his head and captured her mouth in a rough, urgent kiss.

They drank in the taste, the feel, the aroma, of each other, filling their senses to overflowing. The chill of lonely days and tossing and turning nights was pushed aside by the building heat of the desire consuming them. The kiss gentled, so that it could be savored, memorized, tucked away and cherished.

Kurt finally broke the kiss, but kept his tight hold on Dana.

"I missed you," he said.

"I missed you, too."

"I'm glad you were still out here at the house when I arrived."

"I've been staying longer each day. It's so peaceful here, Kurt, so lovely."

Kurt looked at her for a long moment, then slowly, reluctantly, eased her away from his aroused body.

"Ah, Dana," he said, frowning, "what are you doing to me?"

"Only what you're doing to me," she said, then drew a steadying breath. "I don't know, don't understand, what this is that's happening between us." She sighed. "How simple it would be if it was just earthy lust that would burn itself out, but... Oh, Kurt, don't you see? It's the wrong time, the wrong place."

"Why?"

"Because I..." Dana averted her eyes from Kurt's. "I have to find Natalie, remember? As soon as I'm able, I'm leaving Whitehorn so I can continue the search for my sister."

"I can help you find her, Dana. As a cop, I have access to..."

"No." Dana looked directly at him again. "No, this isn't your problem. It's very complicated and would require too much of your time. You have things to do for Sheriff Hensley, and you're supposed to be recuperating, as well, not taking on extra hours of work. No, you mustn't become involved in this situation with Natalie."

Kurt frowned. "Don't you ever get lonely behind there, Dana?"

"Pardon me?"

"Behind that wall you slam into place around yourself when the mood strikes. Doesn't it get lonely?"

Yes! Dana thought. And so frightening.

"No, of course not," she said, lifting her chin. "Why should it? I simply prefer to keep my private problems exactly that...private. I'm certainly not proud of the fact that I have a sister who apparently has no conscience, no regard for anyone but herself.''

"Natalie's behavior isn't your fault."

"No, it isn't." Dana sighed. "But the ramifications of what she has done has had a major impact on my life. I have to find her so everything can be straightened out. Please, Kurt, don't push. I don't want you caught up in this nightmare."

Kurt nodded slowly.

"So!" Dana produced a bright smile. "How was your stay in Billings?"

"Boring. Have you eaten lunch?"

"Yes. I hope you don't mind, but I brought some food out here and put it in your refrigerator. I came early each morning and stayed on. I usually didn't go back to the motel until the middle of the afternoon."

"You haven't made any friends in Whitehorn?"

"What would I say during the chitchat between people who are getting to know each other? I hate to lie. I hate it. And I'm not about to explain that I'm searching for a sister who is like a stranger. A sister who has a disgusting set of values. No, I've avoided contact with the people in Whitehorn as much as possible."

"You must be going stir-crazy."

"I should be, but once I discovered how peaceful and relaxing it was out here, I've been fine. You're so fortunate to have grown up here, Kurt."

"Nice scenery does not an idyllic childhood make, you know."

"Yes, you're right. I'm sorry. It must have been difficult after your father left."

"Yep, but it wasn't all bad. My mother was a good,

decent woman, and my sister, Leigh, and I were close, hung together. I could have lived without my mom being the soup kitchen for every stray cat in the county, though.''

Dana laughed. ''The cats are darlings. Did you know there's one about to give birth to kittens?''

Kurt raised both hands. ''I don't want to hear this. Next thing I know, you'll be telling me to stand by, ready to boil water, or whatever.''

''Don't be silly.'' Dana paused. ''Actually, I was going to try to convince you to let me make a nice birthing box for her and bring her into the house.''

''Oh, no, you don't,'' Kurt said, starting toward the front porch. Dana was right behind him. ''Not on your life. Nope. No way.''

''You're cold, Kurt Noble,'' Dana said. ''How would you like to give birth on a front porch, or under a bush, or something grim like that?''

''I can't say I've given a lot of thought to where I might give birth.''

''You know what I mean.''

Kurt stopped on the porch and stared down at the sleeping pregnant cat.

''Those babies are bowling in there,'' he said. ''Look at that.''

''Isn't it amazing? I call her Mama Kitty. Imagine how a woman must feel when her child, that little miracle, moves within her. It must be so...so awesome, so... I can't even find words to describe the wonder of it.''

Kurt looked directly into Dana's eyes.

''You'll have a baby someday,'' he said. ''You'll experience all that for yourself.''

''I hope so,'' she said softly.

Time stopped. The misty haze of heated desire wove around them once again, encasing them in a cocoon of passion, of racing hearts, of memories of their shared lovemaking. Kurt drew one thumb over Dana's lips, and she shivered at the gentle, tantalizing foray.

Kurt was home, she thought dreamily.

The pregnant cat woke and meowed loudly, stretching her bloated body.

Kurt dropped his hand and cleared his throat.

"Yeah, well," he said, "I appreciate your tending to the beasts while I was gone."

"I enjoyed it," Dana said, her voice not quite steady. "I'd better go in and clear my food out of your refrigerator, so it won't be in your way."

"Dana, look, you can still come out here during the day if you want to. I hate to think that my returning home has sentenced you to long days cooped up in your motel room. I'll be in town working, and you could have the place to yourself."

"That would be wonderful. Thank you."

"Sure."

"Well, I guess I'll be on my way. Welcome home, Kurt. Goodbye."

Dana left the porch and hurried to her car. Kurt watched her go, not moving until her vehicle disappeared from view. He finally switched his gaze to the pregnant cat.

"Mama Kitty, is it?" he said, glaring at the cat. "Cute. But you're still not having that litter in the house."

The cat glared right back at him, then closed her eyes. Kurt muttered an expletive, then entered the house. In the living room, he stopped dead in his tracks.

He could smell Dana's light floral cologne, he thought. It was as though she were still there, in his house, close to him. She'd left her mark on the Noble home.

The fragrance would fade, disappear, as though it had never been there. But Dana herself, the woman? She wouldn't be that easy to forget. She was chipping away at his defenses, caused him to do the exact opposite of what he'd told himself he should and would do.

When he was with Dana, every good intention of putting physical and emotional distance between himself and that captivating woman and her damnable secrets went up in desire-laden smoke.

Kurt's gaze swept over the room, his mind's eye seeing Dana moving through the small expanse, then turning to smile at him as he came through the door.

Welcome home, Kurt.

She'd said that to him while they were standing on the porch.

Welcome home, Kurt.

If Dana was here, waiting for him, this shabby old place would be transformed into exactly that…a home.

"Enough of this," Kurt said, then spun around and left the house, slamming the door behind.

He stepped over Mama Kitty and drove away in a cloud of dust.

Chapter Eight

Three days later, in midafternoon, J. D. Cade entered the Hip Hop Café. He'd driven into Whitehorn to pick up a part for one of the tractors on the Kincaid spread and decided a piece of homemade Hip Hop pie was in order before he returned to the ranch.

He'd buy Freeway a doughnut, too, J.D. decided, glancing around for a place to sit in the crowded café. The dumb dog had done his dramatic deep-sigh routine with such expertise over being left in the truck that he deserved a reward for his performance.

J.D.'s heart did a funny little two-step when he saw Dr. Carey Hall sliding out of one of the booths. Her short, curly blond hair was in fluffy disarray, and she wore khaki slacks with a baggy pink sweater about three sizes too big for her.

J.D. couldn't take his eyes off of her.

Once again, he admitted, seeing Carey Hall made

him feel as though he'd been punched in the solar plexus, making it difficult to breathe.

Why Carey had such an unsettling, sensual impact on him, he had no idea. Yeah, sure, she was pretty enough, in a wholesome, no-nonsense way. She didn't use makeup and wore clothes that gave no hint of what her womanly attributes might be beneath the oversize garments.

Carey was intelligent, as was evidenced by the fact that she was a pediatrician who was held in high regard in Whitehorn, J.D. mused on. Carey's daughter, Sophie, was a cute-as-a-button five-year-old bundle of energy.

He'd heard Winona Cobbs laughing one time about the fact that Sophie Hall had her heart set on finding herself a daddy. Carey Hall, Winona had added, wasn't keen on the idea one iota.

J.D. glanced around quickly in embarrassment as he realized he hadn't moved since entering the café. He'd simply stood there like a lump, drinking in the sight of Carey, who had lingered to chat with someone sitting up at the counter.

Whoa, he thought. Carey was waggling her fingers in farewell and...yes, now she was headed straight toward him. Oh, Lord, she was smiling, and those dimples of hers were enough to cut him off at the knees.

"Good afternoon, J.D.," Carey said, stopping in front of him. "It's nice to see you again."

J.D. touched the brim of his Stetson. "Hello, Carey. It's nice to see you, too." *Brilliant, Kincaid.* He'd sounded like a parrot, echoing her words. "I came in for some pie. Could I interest you in joining me?"

"I just had a slice of coconut cream that was delicious," Carey said, still smiling. "Thank you for the thought, though."

"Could you handle another cup of coffee?" J.D. said. "Or a soft drink? Iced tea?"

"Well, I..."

"J.D.," Janie Carson said, seeming to appear out of nowhere. She splayed one hand on J.D.'s upper right arm. "How are you doing, sugar? The minute I saw you come in, I saved you a slice of chocolate pie. I know that's your favorite. Of course, there are a lot of other things you like far more than chocolate pie. Right, sugar?"

J.D. frowned. "Look, Janie, I..."

"I've got to dash," Carey said, no longer smiling. She scooted around J.D. and Janie. "Bye."

"Bye-bye," Janie said, in a singsong voice.

J.D. removed Janie's hand from his arm as he turned his head to watch Carey hurry out of the café. He looked at Janie again, a frown on his face.

"What was that all about?" he said. "You were acting as though you and I..." He sighed. "Never mind."

"You want the chocolate pie, don't you?" Janie said, beaming at him.

"Yeah, I suppose, and wrap up a doughnut for Freeway. I'll sit up at the counter there."

"You bet," Janie said. "You settle in, and I'll fix you right up." She hurried away.

J.D. slid onto a stool, greeted the man next to him, then scowled at the counter.

If Janie Carson did any more of her famous fixing, he thought, he'd be lucky if Carey Hall even said hello the next time he saw her. Damn.

* * *

At seven o'clock that evening, Dana's head snapped up as a knock sounded at the motel door. She set aside the book she was reading and slid off the bed, padding to the door on bare feet.

"Who is it?" she said, having long since discovered that the door had no safety peephole.

"Kurt."

Dana reached for the chain, then hesitated a moment, ordering her heart to slow its now racing tempo.

All the man had done, she thought with self-disgust, was say his name in that oh-so-sexy voice, and she'd started melting like ice cream in the summer sun. Ridiculous.

Dana squared her shoulders, slipped off the chain and opened the door.

"Hello, Kurt." Her glance fell on the box he was carrying. "You've come bearing gifts?"

"That depends on how you feel about what I'm bringing you. May I come in?"

"Yes, of course," she said, stepping back.

Kurt entered the room and placed the box on the bed. Dana closed the door and went to peer inside the mysterious box.

"Oh, my gosh," she said. "Kittens. Three kittens. But they're so tiny, Kurt. They look like funny little mice."

"Yeah, I know." Kurt dragged one hand through his hair. "Dana, that cat you named Mama Kitty died after giving birth to these three. I couldn't see a thing wrong with her. I guess maybe her heart gave out."

"Oh, no," Dana said. "That's awful, so sad. She was the sweetest thing. Did you bury her in a pretty place?"

Kurt nodded. "There's a nice grove of pine trees

beyond the house. That's the cemetery I've been using for animals since I was a kid."

"Thank you for putting Mama Kitty there, Kurt."

"No problem. The actual problem is these kittens. I talked to the vet and he told me what to do to try to save them. I don't know, Dana, it's going to be a hell of a lot of work, but I figured you'd want them to have a chance at making it."

Kurt paused and shook his head.

"Who am I kidding?" he said. "*I* want them to have a chance, too, believe it or not. Sometimes I think my mother is an angel now, who is looking over my shoulder. She'd have my hide if I didn't do everything possible to save these babies."

Dana smiled. "What a lovely thing to say."

"Yeah, well..." Kurt cleared his throat. "Forget that. The fact is, these kittens have to be hand-fed. I'm not home enough to do it. Do you want the job?"

"Yes, of course. What do I do?"

Kurt took a sack from the box.

"There are special bottles in here, and a bunch of cans of formula. There are several layers of towels in the bottom of the box there, so you can always have a dry, clean one under them.

"Oh, and they eat on demand, not on a schedule. In other words, they're calling all the shots. You should hear the racket they make when they're hungry. Talk about demanding."

"You fed them?"

Kurt nodded. "I was afraid I was going to squish them, because each one looked so small in my hand. I managed to get enough in their stomachs to satisfy them so they'd go back to sleep."

"You never cease to amaze me, Detective Noble."

Kurt laughed. "I have to admit that I rather surprised myself on this one. There I sat, sticking a bottle in the mouth of a kitten that looked like a mouse."

"Mouse," Dana said, tapping one fingertip against her chin. "I like that. I think we should call the one that is all white Mouse. Okay?"

"I wouldn't pick out names for them at this point," Kurt said, frowning

"Why not?"

"They might not make it, Dana. It will be harder on you if they have names, then.... Understand?"

"Yes, but I'll feel badly if they die, even if all I'd ever called them was Kitten One, Two and Three."

"You're a softy."

"Kurt Noble," Dana said, laughing, "so are you. Who contacted the vet, bought these little guys special formula, made them up a crib in a box, then brought them here for tender loving care?"

"Don't tell anyone, for Pete's sake," he said, smiling. "It would blow my macho image."

"Oh? How much is my silence worth to you?"

"Well, let's see." Kurt framed Dana's face in his hands and brushed his lips over hers. Dana shivered. "What can I do to guarantee your silence?" He outlined her lips with the tip of his tongue. Her knees began to tremble. "There must be something."

"You're rotten," Dana said, a catch in her voice.

"You're delicious," Kurt said, then captured her mouth with his.

Kurt was most definitely home, Dana thought, and then all rational thought fled.

The kiss intensified, heightening passions to a heated, feverish pitch. Kurt's tongue delved into

Dana's mouth, and she met it with her own tongue in a seductive duel.

She sank her fingertips into Kurt's thick hair as he dropped his hands from her face to wrap his arms around her, pulling her close.

They were there again, in the field of wildflowers that danced in a fragrant breeze beneath the blue Montana sky.

They were there again, and there was nowhere else they wished to be.

Kurt broke the kiss to enable them to shed their clothes. He moved the box containing the sleeping kittens to the table as Dana placed her books on the nightstand, then swept back the blankets on the bed.

They fell onto the cool sheets, each reaching for the other eagerly, joyfully, in unspoken agreement.

Kurt rested on one forearm, ignoring the ache in his damaged shoulder, as he trailed nibbling kisses along Dana's slender throat. He sought one of her breasts, paying homage to the sweet bounty with his flickering tongue. His hand skimmed over her dewy skin, along her thigh, across the flat plane of her stomach.

Dana's hands roamed over Kurt's muscled back, savoring the masculine contours. She was on fire, the heat of desire consuming her with burning need. Wherever Kurt's lips touched her tingling skin, flames licked into being, hotter, higher.

''Kurt,'' she whispered. ''Please.''

He entered her and began the rocking rhythm that she matched perfectly.

Hotter, higher.

They held back, anticipating, now knowing how

glorious the summit of their climb would be, waiting until they could wait no more.

"Ah, Dana..." Kurt said, and then a groan rumbled deep in his chest.

They were flung into a place far above the wild-flowers. Their place, only theirs. They hovered there, not wishing to return to reality. Slowly, slowly, they drifted back.

Kurt shifted to lie next to Dana. Their heads were on the same pillow, hands resting comfortably, pos-sessively on each other's cooling bodies. Neither of them spoke as they drifted off into sated slumber.

When Dana was jolted awake, the room was dark and the expanse of bed next to her was empty. She blinked several times, wondering foggily what the strange noise was that had brought her from her deep sleep.

"Oh," she said, reaching over to snap on the light. "The kittens. The babies are hungry."

Ten minutes later, Dana sat propped against the pillows on the bed, feeding Mouse with the minuscule bottle.

Absurd, she thought suddenly. If she really looked closely at her present circumstances, the whole sce-nario was absolutely absurd.

She was perched on a rumpled bed in a crummy motel in dinky Whitehorn, Montana, feeding an or-phaned kitten named Mouse.

She was running *away* from the police in Chicago, but at every opportunity ran *into* the arms of a police officer in Whitehorn.

The affair—and there was no other word to de-scribe it—that she was having with Kurt Noble was becoming more and more intense, causing the caring to grow deeper, wrapping itself around her heart.

She still refused to succumb to tears over what Natalie had done to her, what the future might bring because of her sister's hateful actions.

Somewhere down the line, when she allowed herself the luxury of weeping, she hoped to the heavens that a broken heart caused by her foolish involvement with Kurt wouldn't be added to the list of reasons she was crying.

How quickly her life had been changed by the nightmare Natalie created, Dana mused. And yet... Because of the distance standing between what her existence was now and what it had been, she could clearly view her life in Chicago.

She'd been focused on her career with a driving tunnel vision that left room for little else. She had dated occasionally, had been aware of but ignored the fact that Todd Gunderson wanted more from her than casual outings. She felt nothing for Todd beyond friendship.

Growing up in Natalie's vibrant shadow, watching boys, then, later, men, being drawn to her sister's reckless life-style like moths to a flame, had resulted in Dana believing that men weren't interested in a woman of intelligence who was determined to excel in her chosen career. Loving intensely, and being loved in kind, simply wasn't going to happen.

But now there was Kurt.

That an earthy, sensual, masculinity-personified man like Kurt Noble desired her was astonishing...and wonderful. That she responded to his kiss and touch with such abandonment, holding nothing back, was startling...and fantastic.

How to validate your
Editor's FREE GIFT "Thank You"

1. Peel off gift seal from front cover. Place it in space provided at right. This automatically entitles you to receive two free books and a fabulous mystery gift.

2. Send back this card and you'll get brand-new Silhouette Special Edition® novels. These books have a cover price of $4.75 each, but they are yours to keep absolutely free.

3. There's no catch. You're under no obligation to buy anything. We charge nothing—ZERO—for your first shipment. And you don't have to make any minimum number of purchases—not even one!

4. The fact is thousands of readers enjoy receiving books by mail from the Silhouette Reader Service™. They like the convenience of home delivery...they like getting the best new novels BEFORE they're available in stores... and they love our discount prices!

5. We hope that after receiving your free books you'll want to remain a subscriber. But the choice is yours— to continue or cancel, any time at all! So why not take us up on our invitation, with no risk of any kind. You'll be glad you did!

6. Don't forget to detach your FREE BOOKMARK. And remember...just for validating your Editor's Free Gift Offer, we'll send you THREE gifts, *ABSOLUTELY FREE!*

GET A FREE MYSTERY GIFT...

SILHOUETTE®

With our compliments

The Editors

PLA
FREE
SE
HE

YES! I have place

You" seal in the space
send me 2 free books
gift. I understand I am
purchase any books, a
and on the opposite p

Name

Address

City

Province

Thank

019561 9199-L2A5X3-BR01

SILHOUETTE READER SERVICE
PO BOX 609
FORT ERIE ONT
L2A 9Z9

MAIL⟫POSTE
Canada Post Corporation/Société canadienne des postes
Postage paid   Port payé
If mailed in Canada   si posté au Canada

Business   Réponse
Reply   d'affaires

0195619199   01

When she fled from Chicago, Dana thought, she'd shed her straitlaced facade, along with the boredom of her day-to-day life. She was frightened to death of what might become of her if Natalie couldn't be found, but at the same time was excited beyond measure at the discovery of the Dana Bailey within her she hadn't even known was there.

"It's all so crazy, Mouse," Dana said to the kitten, "and so very, very confusing."

The next day Kurt was walking back to the police station after having lunch at the Hip Hop.

"Yo, Kurt," a voice called. "Wait a second."

Kurt turned, a smile appearing on his face as he instantly recognized the man sprinting toward him.

Travis Bains was tall and nicely muscled from the hard work he continually did on his ranch, had sun-streaked brown hair, and was considered an extremely handsome man by the female populace of Whitehorn.

But Travis was not available. He was a one-woman man, who was married to Lori Parker Bains, a highly respected midwife. Lori and Travis had grown up together, married, divorced, then remarried about six years after dissolving their union. They now had three daughters—a toddler, as well as infant twins.

Travis Bains and Kurt Noble had been best friends since they were old enough to walk and talk. The pair shook hands when Travis halted his run in front of Kurt.

"How are you?" Travis said.

"Good, doing good," Kurt said. "How are Lori and your harem?"

"Fantastic. I'll take pity on you and not whip out the wad of pictures I have in my wallet. Lori wants to know why you're being such a stranger. You've only come by the ranch twice since you've been back in Whitehorn.''

"I'll get out there soon. Things have been a bit hectic.''

"Shoulder healing up?'' Travis said.

"Coming along.'' Kurt paused. "Are you in a rush? I have some time left before I'm due back in the office. I'd like to talk to you, Travis.''

"Sure. I was just going to grab a sandwich at the Hip Hop. That can wait. What's on your mind?''

"Let's go sit on that bench under the mulberry over there.''

The two men settled on the wooden bench, each stretching out long legs and crossing them at the ankle. Following the unspoken code of men engaging in a serious discussion, they stared at their toes, instead of looking at each other.

Several minutes passed in silence. Travis waited patiently, knowing Kurt would divulge what was on his mind when he was ready.

"Travis,'' Kurt finally said, "I told you I was shot when an undercover drug bust went momentarily sour.''

"Mmm,'' Travis said.

"What I didn't say was that it was all my fault. Oh, we got the perps, but taking a bullet was due to my own stupidity.''

"That a fact?''

"In spades. While I was undercover during those weeks, I came to know the woman who was involved with the head honcho of the drug ring.'' Kurt frowned and shook his head. "She did a phony number on me, and I bought into it, fell for it big-time.''

"What do you mean?"

"I actually believed that she had gotten swept away by a smooth talker, was in over her head before she realized what had happened. Her 'Oh, poor me' routine was Academy Award material." Kurt laughed, the sound a sharp, harsh bark of self-disgust. "I was going to save her from the scumball who had pulled her under, get her off the drugs she was addicted to."

"Mmm," Travis said.

"Are you ready for this, Travis? I even told her that I was a cop."

"Well, hell, Noble."

"Yeah, I know. I assured her I'd do everything I could for her when the bust was made, get her into rehab, plead her case with my superiors. I was the original knight in shining armor, ad nauseam."

"And?"

"She turned on me at the last minute. It looked like the perps were going to make it out of there, so she went with what she thought was the winning side, hollering her head off that I was a cop. Her sweet patootie shot me, the sleazeball.

"Then our guys came charging in and that was all she wrote. The whole drug ring, including that damnable babe, are in the slammer."

"Well, you didn't die from the bullet wound," Travis said. "Do we have a happy ending here? Except, of course, for the fact that you're still mad as hell at yourself for being suckered by a woman."

"I was a fool."

"Yep, and I was a fool to have lost Lori for a half-dozen years. When I set out to win her back, I had to put the past behind me so I could move toward the future. Are you following what I'm saying?"

"Yeah, and you're right, I know you are, but I'm scared out of my shorts that the past might be repeating itself, in a way."

"What do you mean?"

"Dana Bailey."

"The woman who was involved in that holdup at the convenience store?"

"Yes."

Travis nodded. "I hear she's still in town, been here three weeks now, and is staying out at the Whitehorn Motel so she'll be available to testify at the trial of the guy who shot Clem. Clem is still in a coma.

"What else? Oh, yeah, Dana tended to your cats while you were in Billings, and spends a lot of extra time out at your place when you're not there. She's pleasant enough, very pretty, but keeps to herself."

Kurt chuckled. "Seen Lily Mae Wheeler recently, have you?"

"Yep. Our town gossip is in prime condition. I probably would have been told what Dana eats for breakfast, if I hadn't made my escape from Lily Mae." Travis paused. "Back to business. What does Dana Bailey have to do with what happened with the less-than-lovely woman who got you shot?"

"Dana has secrets, things she's keeping from me, Travis. She can be so open, honest, real, so giving, caring and..." Kurt stopped talking and cleared his throat. "Anyway, she's holding something back, not telling me the complete truth. I swore I'd never again get played for a fool by a woman who wasn't what she appeared to be. Now here I am... What I mean is..."

"Dana is staking a claim on you."

"No. Yes. Hell, I don't know." Kurt dragged both

hands through his hair. "I order myself to keep away from her, that she's trouble in a pretty package. Then there I am, knocking on her door at the motel, or telling her she's more than welcome to hang out at my place as much as she wants to."

"Mmm," Travis said.

"She's got the biggest blue eyes I've ever seen, Travis. The biggest and most beautiful blue eyes, and... Ah, hell, I'm a wreck."

"Yep," Travis said, nodding slowly. "You're definitely losing it, buddy. May I offer you some advice, or was I just supposed to listen and keep my big mouth closed?"

"Whatever," Kurt muttered.

"Well, I'd say that you'd best find out everything you need to know about Dana Bailey, and do it as quickly as possible."

"Why the rush? To save my sanity?"

"It may be too late for that. No, the urgency comes from the fact that you, my man, are going down for the count. You're falling in love with the mysterious Ms. Bailey with the big blue eyes."

"You're out of your mind, Bains," Kurt said, lunging to his feet. "Yes, okay, I care for her, don't have any willpower when it comes to staying away from her, but I never said anything about... Damn it, Travis, I'm not falling in love with Dana."

Travis planted his large hands on his thighs and pushed himself to his feet. He tugged his Stetson low on his forehead and looked directly at Kurt.

"Aren't you?" Travis said quietly. "Are you absolutely positive about that? Think about it, Noble." He turned and started away.

"Go to hell, Bains," Kurt called after him.

Travis raised one hand in farewell and kept on walking.

"That man has slipped over the edge," Kurt said under his breath, as he strode in the direction of the police station. "Well, what do you expect from a guy whose house is overflowing with females? Yep, Travis Bains is nuts. I am *not* falling in love with Dana Bailey."

Kurt covered another ten feet of sidewalk.

"Am I?"

Chapter Nine

Just before five o'clock that evening, Whitehorn was
buzzing.

Clem had come out of the coma!

He'd opened his eyes, said he was hungry, and
asked who was minding the store.

The lawyers involved in the case met immediately
with Judge Kate Randall Walker, and a trial date was
set for one week later. Kimberly typed—slowly—no-
tices to those being summoned to jury duty.

A reporter from one of the large newspapers in Billings had driven off the freeway for the precise purpose of having a delicious dinner at the Hip Hop Café
before finishing his trip home.

No one noticed that Lily Mae Wheeler talked non-
stop to the young man while he consumed his huge
meal. No one heard Lily Mae tell him of Dana Bailey's courageous actions during the attempted holdup

and her admirable willingness to stay on in Whitehorn to be able to testify against the horrible man who had shot their dear Clem.

No one knew that the reporter filed the story with his paper when he arrived in Billings late that night.

Kurt bought hamburgers, fries and thick milk shakes, then drove to the Whitehorn Motel, telling himself that Clem's regaining consciousness and the trial date being set were causes for celebration. He gave Dana the bulletins.

"I don't believe it," Dana said, clasping her hands beneath her chin.

Kurt unpacked the dinner that was filling the small room with mouthwatering aromas.

"It's true," he said. "Absolutely, positively true."

Dana sank onto a chair at the table. "I don't believe it."

Kurt chuckled. "Pick up the phone and call anyone in Whitehorn. The whole town is talking about it."

"I'm so glad that Clem is going to recover. I'll never forget the horror of seeing him shot down like that." Dana smiled. "And there's actually a trial date set for a week from now? That's fantastic."

"Yes, I'm sure that you're pleased," Kurt said, no hint of a smile remaining on his face. He sat down opposite Dana. "You'll be able to leave Whitehorn once you testify, and it's clear that neither attorney plans to recall you to the witness stand. You can ride off into the sunset, exactly the way you've been wanting to."

"Kurt, don't," Dana said, covering one of his hands with one of hers on the top of the table. "Please don't get angry because I'll be leaving. We both knew this was coming. You're not staying in Whitehorn permanently, either, remember? What we began has to end.''

"Is it that easy for you, Dana?'' he said, pulling his hand free. "You were stuck in boring Whitehorn, Montana, so you spiced things up by hopping into bed with a local yokel? Now? Well, thank heavens, you'll be able to split in a week or so.''

The color drained from Dana's face, and pain was reflected in the depths of her expressive blue eyes.

Ah, damn, Kurt thought, look what he'd done. The idea of Dana leaving, of never seeing her again, had hit him hard, like a punch in the gut. An amalgam of emotions had slammed against his mind, as well, all tangled up in a maze.

His own upset and inner turmoil had caused him to lash out at the last person in the world who deserved it. He hadn't meant what he said. He really hadn't. He...

Uh-oh, he thought. The color was returning to Dana's face, and those gorgeous blue eyes were now narrowed and flashing a message as clear as a neon sign. Dana Bailey was mad as hell.

Dana planted her hands flat on the table and rose to her feet, bending over to speak close to Kurt's face.

"How dare you!'' she said, her voice quivering with fury. "I will not stand silently by and allow you to cheapen me *or* what we've shared. I don't give a tinker's damn what you do with the memories of our lovemaking, Kurt Noble, but you will *not* tarnish mine. Is that clear?''

"I...''

"Shut up. No, it won't be *that easy* for me to just get in my car and drive away, leave you, knowing our paths will never cross again. I'm probably going to end up crying over you, and I could come to really hate you for that.'' Dana plunked back down in her chair. "Oh, you're a despicable man.''

"Yeah, I know.'' Kurt sighed. "I'm sorry. Okay? I didn't mean what I said. The thought of your leaving threw me, and... That's no excuse for... But I *am* sorry, and I apologize. Believe me, Dana, I'll be keeping the memories of what we've shared in a very safe place.''

Which did not mean, Kurt mentally tacked on, that he was falling in love with Dana Bailey. Travis Bains was so off base on that, it was laughable. Right? Right. Oh, man, that better be right.

"Oh,'' Dana said.

"Will you accept my apology?''

Dana picked up a fry and nibbled on it while she stared at the ceiling.

"Well?'' Kurt said, frowning.

"I'm thinking it over.''

Kurt burst into laughter. "You're something, you really are. At the risk of getting decked for sounding phony and corny, I have to say this. You're beautiful when you're angry.''

"You're kidding.'' Dana laughed. "That's bottom-of-the-barrel bad. You've really got to get some new material, Detective Noble.''

Their smiles faded slowly as they continued to look directly into each other's eyes.

"I'll miss you very much, Kurt,'' Dana finally said softy.

"I'll miss you, too, lady. I hope you find Natalie and straighten out whatever it is she has messed up.

You might drop me a note, or give me a call, and let me know how it went.''

''Maybe.'' Dana paused. ''Let's not be so gloomy. We've got this sensational celebration dinner to eat. Besides, I'm not leaving for a week or so.''

''True.''

''The kittens are thriving. They sure gobble up that formula. I named them Minnie, Mickey and Mouse. Cute, huh? Oh, dear, we'll have to find someone to tend to them after I...''

''Shh,'' Kurt said interrupting her. ''We're not discussing your leaving Whitehorn anymore tonight. The subject is officially off-limits.''

''All right.'' Dana took a bite of hamburger. ''Mmm.''

They ate in comfortable silence, polishing off the fast-food meal.

''Delicious, and I thank you,'' Dana said, stuffing wrappers in the sack.

''Gourmet to the max,'' Kurt said, helping to clean the table.

''Kurt, let's paint your living room.''

''What?'' he said, rolling up the top of the sack.

''I'm serious. It'll be fun. Your house could be so charming and cozy. I've mentally redecorated it while I've been out there. I wish you could peek into my mind and see everything I've done to it.''

Kurt smiled absently.

He'd definitely like to peek into Dana's mind, he thought, but not to view her plans for his house. He'd give anything to satisfy his lingering doubts, learn exactly what it was that she was still keeping from him.

"I don't think my shoulder is up to slapping paint on walls," he said.

"Oh, heavens, I didn't think of that. Well, I could paint the living room. Would you let me do that? Please? I'd enjoy it so much. It was good of you to let me hang out at your house. I'd like to do you some favor in return."

Kurt shrugged. "Whatever. Go to the hardware store and get what you need. Just tell them I'll stop by later and pay for the stuff. Wouldn't you rather read a book? Painting walls is hard work."

"I'm tired of sitting around on my bottom."

"It's a very nice bottom."

"Thank you, but I'm still tired of sitting on it. This is great. I'll start painting tomorrow."

"My goodness, Ms. Bailey, you're getting all maternal and domestic on me here. You're tending to newborn kittens, and you're about to spruce up a shabby old house. I think you're blowing your image of being a big-city corporate attorney."

"Yes," Dana said, appearing rather pleased with herself, "I guess I am. Sitting here seeing myself in my mind's eye in my power suits, briefcase always at the ready, I look disgustingly stuffy."

Kurt rocked onto the two back legs of the chair and folded his arms over his chest as he smiled at Dana.

"Is that a fact?" he said.

"Definitely stuffy." Dana laughed. "The first year I was gainfully employed as an attorney, I bought a pair of wire-rim glasses that were plain glass, not prescription lenses. I thought they made me look older, more serious and important, the way a lawyer should present herself. Can you believe that? I ended up sitting on the silly glasses by mistake and smashing them to smithereens. I never did figure out how that happened.''

''Don't feel bad. The first time I went undercover as a cop, I grew a beard, thinking I'd look lean and mean. All the beard did was itch like crazy.''

They laughed, the sound of the merry, mingled resonance seeming to fill the room to overflowing.

''You know,'' Dana said, her smile fading slowly, ''I can't picture myself picking up my life where it left off once this nightmare with Natalie is over.''

''No?''

Dana shook her head. ''No. My existence was so narrow, focused entirely on my career. I've changed. I'm not who I was then. I now know that my life in Chicago is too empty, too…lonely.

''I've spent hours walking over the land by your house, Kurt. I've literally and figuratively stopped and smelled the flowers. There's more to have in this world than contracts and corporate mergers, and I want, and need, more now.''

''Such as?'' Kurt said.

His heart was racing, he thought. He could feel it thundering in his chest, and he'd just had to remind himself to breathe. He was waiting for Dana to say she wanted a husband, babies, a home.

Damn it, that was nuts. What difference did it make to *him* what changes she planned to make in her life?

You're falling in love with the mysterious Ms. Bailey with the big blue eyes.

Travis's words beat suddenly against Kurt's brain. He thudded the chair back onto all four legs, hoping the jarring motion would scatter the disturbing message.

''Dana?'' he said, striving for a casual tone of

voice. "What is the *more* that you've decided you now want in your life?"

"What? Oh, sorry. I was daydreaming, I guess, trying to imagine how I could make it work, come together. I want...well, I want it all...a husband, children, a house that is a real home. I'd still like to use my skills as an attorney, but I'd be in charge, call the shots. I'm talking about having my own practice in Chicago, handling the types of cases that I choose to become involved in.

"I'd determine the amount of my workload so I'd have room for other things in my life. But I could never give up the career I've sacrificed so much to have. It means too much to me. I could not, would not, ever walk totally away from the challenge of that arena."

He was going to leap across that table and kiss Dana Bailey senseless, Kurt thought. He was going to shout for joy and maybe turn a cartwheel or two.

What she was saying about her overzealous dedication to her high-powered career wasn't perfect, not by a long shot, but it was a start, a beginning. It was...

Damn it, Noble, get a grip, he ordered himself angrily. This was all Travis Bains's fault. That idiot had declared that Kurt was falling in love with Dana Bailey, and the idiotic statement was doing tricky things to his mind, his ability to reason, think clearly.

"I wonder if that's a pipe dream, not a daydream," Dana said. "Do you think people can really have all that, Kurt? Or is it just too much to ask? Does a person continually fall short in one role or another because they try to wear too many hats?"

"It depends how badly you really want it all, how

hard you're willing to work at it," he said. "Two people, a husband and wife, with the same goals, could make a go of it, I think. Yes, I'm certain they could. They'd compromise, share the load, that sort of thing."

Dana nodded, her eyes riveted on Kurt's face, his blue eyes.

Two people, her mind hummed. A husband, a wife. Kurt and Dana. Babies created by exquisite lovemaking shared. *Their* children, who would be loved beyond measure. A home filled with warmth and laughter.

Oh, Dana, don't do this to yourself.

She was leaving Whitehorn in a week or so, and Kurt would be returning to Seattle when his shoulder was healed completely. They would never see each other again.

Yes, her feelings for Kurt were growing steadily, becoming deeper, more intense. She'd deal with that after she had driven away from Whitehorn, Montana.

She was, foolish as it might be, going to spend as much time as possible with Kurt, share all and everything she could with him, in the days left to her. She was giving, as a gift to herself, those hours and what they would hold.

But to envision the fictitious husband and wife as the two of them? The children as theirs? A house transformed into a home bursting at the seams with love? All that was beyond foolish. It was heartache and tears guaranteed, when she had to face the realization that none of those things would ever come to be.

She had to change the subject, Dana thought, shift

this conversation in another direction, halt the trek down this dangerous road.

"So!" she said brightly. "Do you have a color preference for your living room walls?"

Kurt shrugged. "Surprise me."

"Well, there's something I think you have the right to know."

"Oh?"

Dana burst into laughter. "I've never painted anything in my entire life."

Late the next afternoon, Kurt halted in the doorway of Judd Hensley's office when he saw that the sheriff was talking on the telephone.

After Judd motioned for Kurt to enter, he settled in one of the chairs opposite the desk, crossed his stretched-out legs at the ankle and yawned.

If he sat there too long, Kurt thought, he'd doze off. Not that he was complaining about the lack of sleep he'd had the night before. No way. Not by a long shot.

He and Dana had made love through the hours of the night, reaching for each other over and over again. It had been incredible lovemaking. Beautiful. Fantastic. A combination of the physical and emotional that was beyond description in its intensity and meaning. It had been a night like no other he'd ever experienced. Dana had been so giving, so...

"Am I keeping you from your nap?" Judd said, replacing the receiver of the telephone.

Kurt jerked in the chair. "What? Oh, no, no, I was just thinking about...about what I found at the Kincaid ranch."

"Yeah?" Judd said, raising one eyebrow. "It must

have been quite a find, to produce such a satisfied smile on your face.''

Kurt cleared his throat and straightened in the chair, planting both feet firmly on the floor and ordering the heated coil of desire low in his body that his memories had produced to evaporate *right now*.

''The Kincaid ranch thing,'' he said. ''It was weird, Judd.''

''Fill me in.''

''Parts from one of the tractors had been carefully removed, then laid on the ground in a circle a hundred yards away. Nothing was damaged. Everything was there in that damnable circle.

''It gave me the creeps. It looked like some kind of ritual…you know, a witch's circle, or whatever. Some of the hands out there are really spooked. I bet a couple more of them up and quit on Rand Harding. J. D. Cade was doing his best to help Rand calm those guys down, but…'' Kurt shrugged.

''Were there any clues, any evidence at all that we can work with?'' Judd said.

''Nothing. The tractor parts were wiped clean. The ground was too trampled for any clear footprints. It's just like all the other crazy stuff that has been going on out there. It was carefully executed to give the impression that ghosts, or spirits, or something, are haunting the Kincaid spread.''

''Why?'' Judd said, smacking the top of his desk with the palm of one hand. ''Who is doing this and why? We can't even figure out the motive, let alone who's behind it. Damn, this is frustrating.''

''Yeah, it is. Rand said that Sterling McCallum refuses to fold, won't be beaten by this nonsense. He's not shutting down the ranch.''

"Good for him," Judd said, nodding. "I just wish we were doing a better job for him. We can't patrol a ranch that size and be effective. Besides, we never know where or when the scum will hit. They move all over the spread with no set pattern."

"I know. Things are very tense out there."

"I can imagine." Judd shook his head. "Well, write up a report on what you found and put it in the file with all the others. There's nothing else we can do at this point. Something better break on this…soon."

Kurt nodded, but remained seated.

"Have you got a minute, Judd?" he said.

"Sure. What's on your mind?"

"I've been doing a lot of thinking since I was shot, since I've been home here in Whitehorn. Taking a bullet makes a man look at who he is, where he's going, what he wants."

"Yes, it does."

"I'm not going back on duty in Seattle, Judd. I've had enough of the cloak-and-dagger undercover-cop crap. I'm resigning from the Seattle police force."

"I'll be damned," Judd said, smiling. "I thought you were itching to get back there, to all the excitement and danger. Hell, your life was like one of those cop shows on television."

"Yeah, well, I'm turning off the television set. I've had enough." Kurt paused. "I know Dakota is returning to duty after her maternity leave. The bottom-line question is, do you have room on your force here for me on a permanent basis?"

"You want to stay in Whitehorn?" Judd said, surprise evident on his face.

Kurt nodded. "Yes, I do. I want to be a part of my

niece and nephew's lives as they're growing up, and spend time with my sister and brother-in-law. I want more in my life than just being a cop.''

"Like a wife and family?" Judd said, still smiling. "Hearth and home?"

Yes! Kurt thought. A wife. Babies. A real home, filled with warmth and love.

"Maybe," he said, lifting one shoulder in a shrug. "So? What do you think?"

"I think you're reading my mind," Judd said. "I had coffee with Dakota this morning. She has decided she only wants part-time duty when she comes back. She's not prepared to give up her career entirely, but she doesn't feel she can do justice to being a wife, mother and full-time cop. She prefers to trim down her work hours here."

"And?"

"And I have enough money in the budget to hire you on full-time, with Dakota at part-time. Okay? Is this a done deal?"

Kurt got to his feet. "It is."

Judd rose and extended his hand. "Welcome home, Kurt. It's good to know you're staying on, instead of just dropping by."

"Thanks, Judd," Kurt said, shaking the sheriff's hand. "I appreciate it."

"Hello, hello," Kimberly said, bustling into the office.

"Kim," Judd said, "get together the paperwork to sign Kurt up as a permanent member of the police force and sheriff's department of Whitehorn, Montana."

"Really?" Kim said. "Oh, that's so super." She frowned. "What paperwork?"

"It's in the tall filing cabinet," Judd said.

"It is? Well, I'll find it. Why did I come in here? Oh! Yes! Look at this newspaper from Billings. There's a story about Whitehorn, about Clem being shot and Dana Bailey staying on to testify at the trial and... We made the big-city newspaper. Can you believe that? How do you suppose they found out about an attempted holdup of a convenience store way out here?"

"Let me see that," Kurt said.

Kimberly handed him the newspaper, and Kurt read the story quickly.

"All the details," he said. "My guess is that the reporter came through here."

"And bumped into Lily Mae Wheeler," Kimberly said, laughing.

"That would do it, all right," Judd said, chuckling. "Well, consider that inch of newsprint Whitehorn's fifteen minutes of fame."

"May I keep this paper, Kim?" Kurt said, frowning.

"Sure."

"What's wrong, Kurt?" Judd said. "You don't look too pleased about that story being in the paper."

"It's rather complicated," Kurt said, "and I'd rather not get into it right now, but I think Dana Bailey should see this."

"But why—?" Judd said. Then his telephone rang. He snatched up the receiver

"It's time to go home," Kimberly said, "but I'd better go find that paperwork for you, Kurt, before I forget." She hurried from the room.

Kurt followed Kimberly out of Judd's office, not wishing to be pressed by the sheriff about the newspaper story and Kurt's obvious lack of information regarding his concern about it.

If truth be known, Kurt thought, studying the newspaper as he walked slowly back to his own office, he wasn't all that certain himself why the story had caused a tight knot to twist in his gut.

He entered his office, sat down at his desk and spread out the newspaper, scowling as he stared at it.

Dana was attempting to locate her missing sister, Natalie, he thought. Natalie had done something that had caused problems, trouble, for Dana. Anyone who read the Billings newspaper story now knew exactly where Dana was located.

Was that bad?

Would Dana be upset when she saw the paper, or shrug it off as unimportant?

Would Dana, now, after all they'd shared, finally tell him the complete truth about what was going on?

"There's only one way to find out," Kurt said, getting to his feet.

He picked up the newspaper and strode out of his office, his jaw set in a tight, hard line.

Chapter Ten

Kurt frowned as he drove into the parking lot of the Whitehorn Motel and saw an empty parking place in front of Dana's room.

Had Dana gone out to dinner? he wondered, turning the vehicle around.

He pressed on the brake and folded his arms on top of the steering wheel as he considered his options.

He could wait there for Dana to return. She'd made it clear that she wouldn't be engaging in any lengthy conversations with anyone in town who might ask her personal and probing questions. She shouldn't be gone longer than it took to eat a meal.

Or he could cruise the streets looking for her car, starting by checking at the Hip Hop. He might even join her for dinner, if he found her in time.

"Wait a minute," he said aloud, straightening in the seat.

Dana had planned to paint his living room today. Was she still at his house, slaving over a bucket of smelly paint?

With a mental shrug, Kurt drove out of the parking lot, made one trip through town looking for Dana's car, which he didn't find, then headed for home.

Dana stepped out of the shower in the bathroom in Kurt's house and dried herself with a thin towel. After running her fingers through her freshly shampooed hair, she wrapped another towel around her to create a rather skimpy sarong.

She'd have sworn she'd gotten as much paint on herself as she had rolled onto the living room walls and ceiling, she thought with a smile. She'd practically turned herself into a living statue in Navajo white. But she was pleased with her novice efforts as a housepainter. The living room looked splendid.

And now she was squeaky-clean, and her clothes should be ready to be transferred from the washing machine to the dryer. She'd tossed in her bra and panties for good measure. The small load of wash shouldn't take too long to dry, and she'd be dressed again before Kurt arrived home.

Humming softly, Dana left the steamy bathroom and padded barefoot down the hall.

"Oh, my God!" she yelled, when she entered the living room.

Kurt was standing just inside the front door.

"What are you doing here?" she said, still set on full volume.

"I live here, remember?" Kurt said.

He slid his gaze over Dana, slowly, very slowly,

from the top of her head to the tip of her toes, then retracing the visual journey.

"Stop that." Dana tucked the corner of the towel more firmly into place. "You're undressing me with yours eyes, you cad."

Kurt chuckled. "Cad? That's good, very Victorian. As for undressing you with my eyes you're right. However, if I'm going to do something, I like to give it my maximum effort. Therefore, I'm going to come over there and remove that towel with my hands."

"Don't you dare," Dana said, pointing one finger at him. "Oops," she added as the towel began to slip down. "I wasn't expecting you so soon. I was covered in paint, you see, so I took a shower and washed my hair. My clothes are in the washing machine, and I need to put them in the dryer so they can... Darn it, Kurt, quit staring at me."

"Okay, I'll quit staring at you."

Kurt started across the room toward her, his gaze locked with hers.

A sleek panther, Dana thought giddily. That was what Kurt looked like. He was moving with that lazy grace of his, that masculine, loose-hipped way he had, and he was coming for her, the prey.

A chill coursed through Dana. The shiver was caused partly by the dropping temperature of the evening air. And partly by a flicker of trepidation as Kurt came closer and closer. And partly by anticipation and excitement, with the added wish that he'd hurry up and get there.

Kurt stopped directly in front of her, his eyes having changed from blue to smoky gray, radiating desire, searing her skin like licking flames.

"Do...do you like how the room looks freshly

painted?'' Dana said, hardly recognizing the breathy sound of her own voice.

''Mmm,'' Kurt said, his eyes riveted on hers. ''You did a fantastic job. It's nice, very nice, looks bigger. The room appears twice as big.''

''Yes, I noticed that myself. That it seemed bigger. The room. I covered all the furniture with tarps. The floor, too. I was the only casualty, as far as getting splattered with paint.''

''But now the paint is washed away and your skin is moist, like it's shimmering with morning dew,'' Kurt said, his voice seeming to drop an octave. ''Dew on a soft petal of a lovely flower.''

''Oh, good Lord,'' Dana said, her knees beginning to tremble. ''Kurt, if you don't kiss me or something, I'm going to dissolve into a heap on the floor.''

He brushed his lips over hers.

''Let's go for the 'or something.'''

''Good idea,'' Dana whispered.

''Mmm.''

Several hours later, Dana was dressed in her clean, dry clothes. She and Kurt sat at the kitchen table, finishing a dinner of scrambled eggs and toast.

They'd left the front and back doors open, with the screen doors closed, to keep out the bugs while allowing the crisp breeze to whisk away the lingering odor of paint. Crickets serenaded them while they ate.

Minnie, Mickey and Mouse had been fed and were snoozing in their box by the back door.

Well, Noble? Kurt thought. *How long are you going to postpone showing Dana the newspaper from Billings?*

He sighed inwardly.

The newspaper was still in the pocket of his sport coat, where he'd tossed it over a chair in the bedroom. For two cents, he'd leave it right there, do nothing to spoil these fantastic hours he was spending with Dana.

When she entered the living room clad in nothing more than that scrap of damp, clinging towel, desire had exploded within him. To him, she had looked more beautiful, more tantalizing and alluring, than any woman who might be wearing a fancy, expensive dress for a night on the town.

The room had been a jumbled mess of tarp-covered furniture, paint buckets, brushes, rollers and trays.

The room had been a field of wildflowers.

The heavy odor of paint had hung in the air.

Dana had smelled like fresh air, sunshine, soap and woman.

His woman.

His Dana.

And they'd made love. Exquisite love, beautiful love, among the fragrant flowers that were theirs alone to share.

But now? It was reality-check time. He had to come down out of the sensual, yet contented, cloud he was still hovering in and produce the damnable newspaper story for Dana to read.

"So what do you think?" Dana said. "Should I paint the... Kurt?"

"What?"

"Are you awake?" she said, smiling.

"Judd asked me something like that today, too. He wanted to know if he was keeping me from my nap. I simply told him that I hadn't gotten much sleep last night because I'd spent hours making love with you."

"Oh, you did not say that." Dana's eyes widened. "Did you?"

"No," he said, laughing.

"One never knows what men might divulge to each other when in their male-bonding mode," Dana said, wrinkling her nose. "It's very weird."

"You're an expert on male bonding, are you?"

"I read a lot."

"Mmm. Actually, I was in Judd's office to report on what I'd discovered out at the Kincaid ranch and to…well, to ask him if he had room on the force to hire me on permanently."

Dana opened her mouth to respond to what Kurt had said, then stopped and shook her head before trying again.

"I was actually speechless for a moment there," she said. "I thought that was just something people said in the movies, but it didn't really happen. You're going to quit the Seattle police force? Move back here, live in Whitehorn?"

"Yes."

Dana sank back in her chair and stared at Kurt with wide eyes.

"My goodness," she said, "that is quite an announcement to make out of the blue."

"You're not the only one who has changed, Dana, who wants more out of life than what there was before. Like you, I had to step away from my existence to see how empty it was, how…how lonely it was."

"And this *more* that you want? You believe that it's in Whitehorn?"

"Well, it's a start. I have family here."

"Yes, that's true," she said, nodding. "I envy you that."

Kurt pushed his plate away and folded his arms on the top of the table.

"Dana, you asked me if I thought a person could have it all...be married, have children, a career. I said I believed it could be done if the major players really worked at it together. Well, I want it all, the whole nine yards."

A warmth suffused Dana, tiptoeing first around her heart, then filling her entire being to overflowing. It wasn't the heat of simmering desire, not this time. It was the warm flush of ultimate joy, of sudden happiness that was like nothing, *nothing,* she'd felt before.

Oh, Dana, don't, she admonished herself quickly. That she and Kurt wished to change the course of their lives, were viewing the same path as being where they wished to go, didn't mean they were going to travel that road together.

That wouldn't happen, it couldn't. She had to leave Whitehorn, find Natalie, clear her name of the criminal charges hanging over her head.

And if Natalie couldn't be found? Dear God, she didn't even want to consider such a horrible possibility. She'd be in jail, having been convicted of a crime she had not committed.

Oh, how glorious it would be to pour out her troubles to Kurt, share the nightmare, lean on him a bit for comfort and support. But she wouldn't do that to him. It wasn't fair. The dilemma she was in was hers to solve, to set to rights. Kurt deserved better than to be dragged through the ugly mud that Natalie had created.

She would leave Whitehorn, Montana. Kurt would remain in Whitehorn, Montana. He'd marry a woman, maybe someone he'd grown up with, and they'd have babies. Would they live in this house? Fix it up, so pretty and perfect? Walk hand in hand over the surrounding land and pick a vibrant bouquet of wildflowers?

She hated it. The scenario she was envisioning in her mind of Kurt and another woman was more than she could bear. She was being selfish, she knew it, but right now she didn't care. For the remaining days and lovemaking nights that she had left in this town, Kurt Noble was *hers*.

"Well," she said, producing a small smile, "I wish you every best, Kurt. I hope you fulfill your hopes, your dreams. My, my, isn't it great that I painted the living room? Since you'll be staying on here, it will be nice to have a sparkly-clean front room, don't you think? What about the kitchen? Should I tackle that next, or—"

"Dana…"

"No," she said, getting to her feet. "Whatever you were going to say…just don't. I'm attempting to be so sophisticated and mature, handle all this, and I'm hanging on by a thread. I care for you, Kurt, so very much, but I'm not free to think about anything except finding Natalie."

"Then let me help you do that," he said, his voice rising.

"No, no, no," she said, shaking her head. "You mustn't become involved in this."

"Why not?" He shoved back his chair and got to his feet. "I care for you, too. You know that, don't you? Ah, hell, of course you do. We could work together on this mess you're in, then see where we're headed, or not headed, without whatever your night-mare is hovering over us.''

"No. I have to do this alone, quietly, out of sight. I'm assuming Natalie has no idea I've left Chicago to search for her. If you use your police connections to help me, there's too great a chance that she'll find out that I'm here, and not where she believes I am.''

And the authorities would know that Dana Bailey was in Whitehorn, Montana, too, she thought franti-cally. They would come for her, arrest her, and… No!

"Your cover is already blown, Dana.''

"What? What do you mean?''

"I'll be right back.''

Kurt left the room, and Dana pressed her fingertips to her now throbbing temples.

Oh, why did reality have to ruin such a perfect day? she thought. And what did Kurt mean by saying her cover was already blown?

Kurt reentered the kitchen, a deep frown on his face.

"This is one of the evening newspapers from Bil-lings,'' he said, handing it to her. "You'd better take a good look at it.'' He tapped the center of the paper.

Dana shifted her eyes to the newspaper and began to read the story. Her breath caught and the color drained from her face as black dots danced before her eyes.

"No,'' she whispered, sinking back onto the chair. "Dear heaven, no. Who did this? Who told the re-porter that I'm here, that I'm…''

She looked up at Kurt, a stricken expression on her pale face.

"This can't be happening. Tell me I'm asleep, that I'll wake up and… I have to leave Whitehorn now, tonight. I have to go, because... Yes, I'll disappear before... Oh, God, I can't stay here. I..."

Kurt gripped Dana's upper arms and hauled her to her feet. The newspaper fluttered unnoticed to the floor.

"Stop it," he said, giving her a small shake. "What's the matter with you? I didn't know if you'd be upset by the story in the newspaper or not, but I certainly didn't expect a reaction as extreme as this. Talk to me, Dana. What in the hell is going on?"

The police will know where I am! Dana's mind screamed. They'd track her down, arrest her, take her away and put her in jail before she could find Natalie.

"Natalie...Natalie will realize I'm looking for her," she said, her voice trembling, "if word reaches her about what is in that newspaper. She'll go even deeper into hiding. I have to leave. I have to find my sister."

"Would you calm down and think a minute?" Kurt said, still holding her arms. "Natalie isn't stupid, is she? Wouldn't she have already figured out you'd be searching for her, if she's the key to clearing up whatever trouble she has caused for you?"

"Well, yes, I suppose she would realize I wasn't just throwing up my hands and allowing things to remain as they are."

"So what difference does it make if she knows you're in Whitehorn, Montana? It may even help the situation. You have a detective working on this case, remember? If Natalie thinks you're stuck in Whitehorn until the trial, she may get sloppy, go out in public more, make a mistake, and your guy can nab her...wherever she is."

"Yes, I see what you're saying, but it's not that simple. You just don't understand, Kurt."

Kurt dropped his hands from Dana's arms.

"Then why don't you explain it to me?" he said, a pulse beating wildly in his temple. "What did Natalie do, Dana? Exactly what kind of trouble are you in? Don't you think it's time I knew the whole story, the complete truth?"

Dana shook her head. "No. No, I won't have you involved in this."

"Is that a fact?" he said, a rough edge to his voice. "You make love with me, have said you care deeply for me, know I care for you. You *trust* me with you, the woman, in bed, know I would never harm you. But then you stop, put up that damnable wall of yours and shut me out."

"I have to!" Dana said, nearly shrieking.

Kurt took a deep breath and stared up at the ceiling for a long moment, reining in his building anger and frustration. He blew out a puff of air and looked at Dana again.

"All right," he said, raising both hands palms out. "We'll leave it at that for now. So take your pick. Do you want to spend the night here with the odor of paint, or shall we go back to the motel?"

"What are you talking about?"

"I'm not letting you out of my sight, Dana Bailey," he said, narrowing his eyes. "In the frame of mind you're in at the moment, I'm afraid you're going to take off at the first opportunity. Well, guess what, lady? That isn't going to happen."

"But…"

"I'm a member of the police force of Whitehorn. I'm electing to stand guard over you because you're now a hostile witness of sorts. You *will* testify at that trial, because Clem deserves to have the scum who shot him put behind bars. Are you getting this? Am I making myself perfectly clear on the subject?''

"You can't treat me like a prisoner!"

"You're not giving me any choice but to do exactly that."

They glared at each other, the tension between them a nearly palpable entity, crackling through the air.

"What about your reputation?" Dana said finally. "Word will get around town very quickly that we're spending the nights together. You plan to stay on in Whitehorn permanently. Do you want people gossiping about you like that?"

"I don't give a rip, but to keep my sister from being embarrassed, or put in an uncomfortable position of trying to defend my actions, I'll nip the speculation in the bud."

"Oh, really? How? Take out an ad in the Whitehorn newspaper stating that you're not my lover, you're my jailer?"

"No, I'll simply tell Lily Mae Wheeler that you decided to leave town before testifying on Clem's behalf, and I decided you really shouldn't do that. Lily Mae gets the message out better than any newspaper that has been printed anywhere."

"Oh, you just think of everything, don't you, Detective Noble?" Dana said, planting her hands on her hips. "You have all the answers."

Kurt dragged one hand through his hair.

"No," he said quietly, "I don't. I have a lot more questions than I do answers. Question—what did your twin sister do? Question—what kind of trouble are you in?

"Question—why do you only trust me up to a point, then shut me out? Question—what am I going to do about the fact that you mean so damn much to me and I don't seem to be able to do anything about those emotions? No, Dana, I don't have all the answers. Not by a long shot."

"Oh, Kurt, I'm sorry," she said softly. "You'll never know how badly I feel about all this. It truly is a nightmare, and I'm terrified about the way it might end. Why can't *you* trust *me?* Why can't you believe me when I say I just can't tell you everything now?"

"Because it doesn't work that way," Kurt said wearily. "It just doesn't." He paused. "Let's get out of here. The smell of paint is giving me a headache. We're spending the night at the motel."

It was a long, seemingly endless night.

They drove into Whitehorn in total, stony silence. At the motel, they prepared for bed, still not speaking, then moved as far to the opposite sides of the bed as possible.

Sleep was elusive, each of them acutely aware of the stiff, tense person across the space between them. Each of them remembering the exquisite love they'd made in that bed in the past.

Dana finally dozed in a restless slumber, only to be awakened by the hungry, squeaking kittens. She carried the box into the bathroom and shut the door so that the light wouldn't disturb Kurt.

But Kurt wasn't sleeping. He was so tense his muscles ached and his injured shoulder throbbed in a painful cadence. Thoughts tumbled through his mind, one after another, faster and faster, creating a tangled maze of confusion.

And all the questions were there, taunting him, beating against his brain, shouting the depressing message that he had no answers.

All the questions that were focused on Dana.

At dawn's light, Kurt rose and dressed. Dana watched him from beneath her lashes, then made no pretense of being asleep when Kurt picked up the receiver to the telephone and punched in some numbers.

"Yeah, this is Kurt," he said into the receiver. "I want a patrol car stationed outside Dana Bailey's room at the Whitehorn Motel right away. It's the last room in the row. Ms. Bailey is not to leave. I'll clear it with Judd later." He replaced the receiver.

"You can't do that," Dana said, sitting bolt upright in bed. She wore a T-shirt and panties, but still clutched the sheet beneath her chin.

"I just did," Kurt said, heading for the door.

"How could I go anywhere? My car is still out at your house."

Kurt stopped, his hand on the doorknob, and turned halfway to look at her.

"Travel buses come through Whitehorn. There are also truckers who sometimes come off the highway to have a meal. I imagine you could bat your big blue eyes and come up with a sad enough story to convince one of them to take you with them."

"You honestly believe I'd do something like that?" Dana said incredulously.

"Dana, I'm so dead tired I don't know what to believe right now. All I *do* know for certain is that you are nearly frantic about wanting to leave White-horn, and I'm not going to allow that to happen.'' He turned and yanked open the door. ''Have a nice day.''

Kurt slammed the door closed behind him, and Dana jerked at the loud noise. She flopped down onto the pillow and sighed, her utter fatigue, both physical and emotional, seeming to crush her.

She had to telephone Pete Parker, she thought frantically, and tell the detective about the story in the Billings newspaper. No, it was too early in the morning. Pete wouldn't be in his office yet.

Dana looked over at the pillow where Kurt's head had rested beside her own through the long night.

Just when she'd been convinced that her life couldn't be in a worse mess, she thought miserably, it was actually in a worse mess. Now Kurt, her Kurt, was so furious, so hurt, because she was continuing to keep secrets from him.

On top of everything else she had to deal with, was she also to lose the last precious days, hours, minutes she had left with Kurt Noble? Would he remain so angry, cold and distant?

Dana, please, get in touch with reality, she admonished herself. Kurt's frame of mind was not the priority-one issue she should be concentrating on. She had to figure out a way to leave this town before the Chicago police were informed that fugitive Dana Bailey was hiding out in Whitehorn, Montana.

''Ohhh,'' she said, covering her face with her hands.

She was so tired. Maybe if she slept until she was able to telephone Pete, things would look a bit brighter, wouldn't seem so completely overwhelming and hopeless.

She dropped her arms heavily onto the bed.

Yes, some sleep, she thought foggily. Some sleep.

Dana slept, one hand resting on Kurt's pillow.

After waiting outside for the patrol car to arrive at the motel and repeating his instructions to the uniformed officer behind the wheel, Kurt drove home to shower, shave and change clothes.

When he entered his living room, he stopped, his gaze sweeping over the painting supplies and the fresh, clean ceiling and walls.

The odor of paint was gone. Kurt told himself that it was impossible that he could smell the delicate aroma of Dana's cologne.

Dana had done a fine job, he thought, especially considering that she'd never attempted the chore before. If this house was spruced up room by room, it would be a pretty decent place to live.

But would it ever really be a home?

"Noble, shut up," he said aloud, as he stepped over the painting supplies. "Don't think. Just clean up your decrepit body. Oh, yeah, and feed the blasted cats."

The shower and shave helped him discover a reservoir of energy that had been hidden beneath his mental and physical fatigue. Three cups of coffee and six slices of toast and peanut butter helped him find some more.

Kurt cleaned the kitchen, the clutter including the dishes from the dinner he'd shared with Dana the previous night. He then folded the tarps and took them, along with the other sundry painting supplies, to the shed beyond the back door.

The front room looked really good, he thought,

viewing it minus the working materials. Add new carpeting and furniture, and it would be a comfortable place to settle in for the evening.

But would this house ever be a home?

"Here I go again," he said, throwing up his hands. "I can't stay sane for five minutes at a stretch. I'm outa here."

Behind the wheel of his vehicle, he turned the key in the ignition, but didn't back out of the driveway. He glanced over at Dana's car and frowned.

He was in no rush to go to the police station and see Judd, he admitted. It was still early, but Judd often was the first one in. There was a very good chance that the sheriff would be sitting behind his desk, waiting to hear Kurt's explanation for assigning an officer to make certain that Dana Bailey didn't leave her motel room.

Kurt muttered an earthy expletive.

He didn't want to divulge Dana's personal business to Judd Hensley, then have to confess that he, detective extraordinaire Kurt Noble, had more questions than answers regarding Dana Bailey.

Nor did he wish for the very savvy and perceptive sheriff to pick up on the fact that Kurt was up to his tired eyes in emotional-involvement problems with the secretive woman.

No, he could go all week without having that conversation with Judd. He couldn't put it off that long, but he sure could postpone it for a couple of hours.

Kurt backed out of the driveway and headed for Winona Cobbs's Stop 'N' Swap, knowing she would have risen very early to feed her chickens.

He needed some of Winona's homemade honey,

Kurt told himself. He had no other reason to drive all the way out there. It was a simple fact that peanut butter toast just wasn't what it should be without Winona's honey dribbled on top.

Chapter Eleven

When Kurt arrived at Winona's, she was sitting outside of her mobile home, drinking hot tea laced with
honey made by the bees she kept. The ceramic mug
was decorated with perky bumblebees wearing top
hats.

Kurt waved, then began to make his way through
the clutter. Winona's treasures consisted of everything
a person might want, or would never consider own-
ing, or didn't know even existed.

Kurt stepped around a dented tuba, over a long
wooden window box containing cracked, dry dirt and
dead geraniums, and through a short aisle edged with
various sizes of metal milk cans.

His glance fell on a small round table covered in a
selection of china figurines. He stopped and picked
up one that had two kittens curled next to each other
as they slept. One kitten was white, the other was

white with black ears. The figurine was tiny and delicate, fitting into the palm of his hand with room to spare.

He was going to buy this for Dana, Kurt decided. It would be a peace offering of sorts. He was angry and hurt that Dana still refused to totally confide in him. He guessed that Dana felt angry and hurt because he was having her guarded twenty-four hours a day so that she wouldn't leave town before testifying at the trial.

Heaven knew that a china figurine of sleeping kittens wouldn't mend all the fences between them, but maybe it would pave the way to enabling them to call some kind of truce. It was worth a try.

When Kurt reached Winona, she waved him into the lawn chair next to hers and asked if he'd like some tea.

"No thanks," he said. "I just finished breakfast. I'm going to buy this little figurine, and I also need a quart of honey."

"You must be having peanut butter toast for breakfast, if you want a jar of my honey," Winona said, smiling. "You've liked that combination since you were a sassy little tyke. Oh, I heard you're staying on for good in Whitehorn. I think that's fine, Kurt, mighty fine. Welcome home."

"Mmm," Kurt said, nodding.

"You look tired."

"Yeah, well, I haven't had much sleep in the last couple of nights." Kurt paused. "By the way, Winona, the vision you had of Dana Bailey having two faces was because she has an identical twin sister."

"Is that a fact? Well, that certainly does explain why I saw the faces side by side, not layered. Twins.

Well, isn't that something? So, tell me, Kurt, what brings you all the way out here so early in the morning?''

Kurt frowned. ''I just told you. I need a quart of honey.''

''Being out of honey doesn't explain why you're troubled. And you *are* troubled, dear. I can feel it coming from you in waves of tension, stress.''

''I fooled myself into believing I came only for honey,'' Kurt said, ''but there's no putting anything past you, Winona.'' He stared up at the blue Montana sky for a long moment, then looked at Winona again. ''It's Dana.''

''She's a pretty thing, isn't she?'' Winona said. ''I can't remember when I've seen such big blue eyes as she has. I imagine her feelings show in those eyes.''

''Yes, they do,'' Kurt said. Desire. Merriment. Anger. Pain. Yes, Dana's emotions were clearly reflected in her gorgeous, expressive eyes. ''And, yes, I agree that she's very pretty.''

''Are you in love with Dana Bailey, dear?'' Winona said gently.

''I don't know, Winona. Love is just so damn complicated. I'm not certain that I'd recognize it if it hit me with a brick.''

''Yes, you would, if you weren't fighting not to see it for what it was. People do that, you know, when they're skittish about falling in love.''

''Try scared out of my shorts,'' Kurt said dryly. ''I've made some heavy-duty mistakes in that arena in the past.''

''The past is gone. The future is what's important. The day we're living, and the future days to come, are what count.''

"It's not always easy to forget the past."

"No," Winona said, "but if you allow it to own a part of you, you won't be able to fully savor the present and future." She reached over and grasped Kurt's hand, where it rested on the arm of his chair. "You think about that, dear. You're coming home to Whitehorn, starting fresh and…"

Winona stopped speaking and stared into space.

"Winona?" Kurt said, feeling his heartbeat quicken. "Are you seeing something? Are you having a vision?"

Winona's grip on Kurt's hand tightened, but she didn't speak. Kurt watched her intently, hardly breathing. Thirty seconds became sixty, then ticked slowly by to a minute and a half. Then Winona blinked and shook her head slightly. She released Kurt's hand and sank back in her chair.

"Winona?" Kurt said anxiously.

"Oh, my," she said, then drew a steadying breath.

"What did you see?"

"It was Dana," Winona said, meeting Kurt's troubled gaze with a matching one of her own. "The two faces of Dana."

"Dana and Natalie, her twin sister."

"And danger…dark, dark, danger."

A chill swept through Kurt.

"Danger?" he said. "For who? Dana or Natalie?"

"I don't know. They have the same face. It could be both of them, or just one. I have no way of telling."

Kurt lunged to his feet and began to pace, his fingers curling around the china kittens.

"Danger," he repeated. "I'd wonder if the trouble that Natalie has caused meant that Dana was in danger, then I'd push the thought away, time and again. But, damn it, is it Dana or Natalie who is threatened in some way?''

''You'd best find out, Kurt. In the meantime, I trust you're going to watch over Dana?''

''Guaranteed. I've got to get into town.''

Winona stood. ''I'll get your honey. And, Kurt? Listen to the whispers from your heart, dear.''

''What?''

''Your heart will tell you if you're truly in love with Dana. You must remember to listen.''

''I will, Winona,'' he said, kissing her on the cheek. ''Thank you for everything.''

As Winona went to fetch the honey, Kurt opened his hand and stared at the china kittens.

Nothing, he thought fiercely, was going to happen to his Dana. *Nothing.*

''You're pushing the letter of the law, Kurt,'' Judd Hensley said, smacking the top of his desk with one hand. ''You've literally put Dana Bailey under house arrest, and you can't do that. She's not the perp, she's an eyewitness, for cripe sake.''

''I know, I know,'' Kurt said, raising both hands in a gesture of peacemaking.

Kurt stood opposite Judd's desk, having been summoned to the sheriff's office the moment he arrived in the building.

''But we're just a few days away from going to trial, Judd. Everyone in Whitehorn, including me, wants that creep who shot Clem sentenced to a long prison term. We need Dana to testify.''

''Which she agreed to do. Why is she suddenly determined to leave town?''

"She has family business to attend to that she feels has been put on the back burner for far too long, considering she has been in Whitehorn nearly a month now."

Judd frowned. "We're walking a very fine legal line here. She was told to stay put in Whitehorn, and she has. But to restrict her movements, take away her freedom, treat her like a prisoner under guard, is crossing way over that line."

Kurt folded his arms on his chest and matched Judd's frown.

"What would you suggest I do?" Kurt said. "If we don't watch Dana twenty-four hours a day, she's going to split. I don't know exactly what the family problem is. Her twin sister has done something to cause Dana a lot of trouble." And Dana or Natalie was in danger. Or maybe both of them were. "She's trying to find her sister."

"Okay," Judd said, nodding. "We have resources available for that. Dana stays in Whitehorn, and you use your official police connections to see if you can locate her sister."

"Dana doesn't want me to do that," Kurt said. "I've offered, believe me. She's adamant about me not being swept up in her personal problems, even though we're... What I mean is... Ah, hell..." He rolled his eyes heavenward.

"Oh, great, just great," Judd said, narrowing his eyes. "This is really dandy. You're involved with Dana Bailey. You're emotionally—and since you're both consenting adults, you're probably physically, as well—involved with that woman."

"So sue me," Kurt said, dragging one hand through his hair.

"Damn it, Kurt!"

"Look, I didn't set out to have this happen. Lord knows I've paid a heavy enough price for something like this in the past. But it *did* happen. Okay? I can't change that, Judd. I care a lot for Dana, I really do.

"Dana is in some kind of trouble, deep trouble, and I want to move heaven and earth to fix it. I've respected her wishes up to now to keep my nose out of it, but..."

Kurt shook his head and slouched into one of the chairs opposite Judd's desk. Judd hooked one hand on the back of his neck and stared into space, obviously deep in thought.

Seconds ticked into minutes.

"All right," Judd said finally. "Try this. I've got to call off that uniform you've got sitting outside Dana's motel room. We're over the legal line on that."

"Mmm," Kurt said, a scowl on his face.

"I'm unofficially assigning you to keep tabs on Dana Bailey. You'll be with her as a man, not an officer of the law. I'm not having this case end up in a mistrial that was caused by a technicality and lose that scum who shot Clem. Understood?"

"I hear you," Kurt said glumly. "However, Dana is mad as hell at me at the moment, for keeping her under guard. I'm the last man on earth she'll want hanging around."

"That's *your* problem, Noble. Apologize. Buy her flowers. Grovel, if you have to. She's still under direct orders from me to be available for that trial. The tricky part is to not curtail her freedom as a citizen in the meantime."

"Easy for you to say. She definitely wants to hit the road."

"See that she doesn't." Judd paused. "Kurt, are you in love with Dana?"

"Damned if I know," Kurt said, getting to his feet. "Travis is convinced that I am. Winona says I'm supposed to listen to the whispers from my heart to get the answer to that question. Me? I'd like to sleep for five years and forget the whole mess."

Judd chuckled. "Women. It doesn't matter how big and strong we men are, those little ladies can cut us off at the knees and make scrambled eggs out of our brains."

"You've got that straight."

"But you know something, Kurt?" Judd said seriously. "Men like you and me need the love of a good woman. We need their gentleness and their wisdom. If you're in love with Dana, don't fight it. It could be the best thing that ever happened to you."

"I don't know, Judd. There are just too many questions without answers right now."

"Then start finding the answers."

Dana sat on the bed, her arms wrapped around drawn-up knees as she replayed in her mind the telephone conversation she'd had earlier with Pete Parker.

"Just calm down, Dana," Pete had said. "You're overreacting. The chance of Natalie or the Chicago cops getting wind of a short article with your name mentioned in a Billings, Montana, newspaper is slim to none. Take my word for it, the cops aren't going to come into Whitehorn with guns blazing to arrest you."

"Could you lose the reference to guns blazing? My nerves are stretched to the limit as it is."

Pete had chuckled. "Sorry." He paused. "Are you together enough now to hear some good news? Natalie used one of your charge cards in a hotel in Detroit."

"Really? How do you know that?"

"Hey, if I told you how I find out things, you wouldn't need to keep me on the payroll. You'd do your own detective work. Anyway, I'm flying to Detroit tonight to see what I can dig up."

"Do the Chicago police know about the charge slip?" Dana had said.

"Yep, which is another reason you don't have to panic about a blurb in a Montana newspaper at the moment. They've got a hot lead in another direction as to your whereabouts."

"They're still after *me,* instead of Natalie."

"All that will come out in the wash when I find your sister. You sit tight. I'll keep in touch. See ya."

"Goodbye, Pete."

Dana had sighed.

Hours had passed since that conversation with Pete Parker. She'd had ample time to mentally relive her hysterical performance upon first seeing the story in the newspaper.

It was no wonder Kurt had placed her under guard. She'd given the impression that she was about to go tearing off down the interstate on foot, if need be.

"Oh, dear," Dana said aloud. "I think I need to apologize to Kurt."

She continually hurt Kurt, she knew, by refusing to tell him what he wanted to know regarding the trouble she was in. She hated seeing that flicker of pain in his blue eyes when she stood her silent ground on the subject. No decent woman wished to hurt the man she might very well be falling in love with.

Dana sighed again.

She always hedged when mentally squaring off against her growing feelings, her deepening emotions, for Kurt. She had no desire whatsoever to address the issue of exactly how she felt, or what was happening between them.

What if she discovered that she truly loved Kurt Noble? It would only serve to make her leaving Whitehorn more heartbreaking. It was going to be bad enough as it was, with her admitting that she cared very, *very* much for Kurt.

Kurt. Dear heaven, what would he think of her if he knew she was a fugitive from the law? That she was presumed to be guilty of a high-tech crime? Would he listen to her, allow her to explain, believe that she was an innocent victim of Natalie's duplicity?

She didn't know what Kurt would do, or think, if he knew the truth, and she wasn't planning on finding out.

A knock sounded at the door. Dana pulled herself from her troubled thoughts and slid off the bed.

It was probably her police-officer warden, she thought, inquiring about suggestions for dinner. They'd had a pizza delivered for lunch, and shared it while engaging in a pleasant, albeit bland, conversation. Then the officer had crawled back into his patrol car and stared at her door for the remainder of the afternoon.

Dana opened the door, her eyes widening in surprise.

"Kurt." She looked past him and saw that the patrol car was gone. "Come in."

Kurt entered the room without speaking. Dana closed the door and turned to face him.

"I…" she said.

"Dana…"

They spoke at the same time, then stopped, looking directly into each other's eyes.

"Go ahead," Kurt said. "My mother taught me that ladies are always first."

"Well, I'm not sure I qualify, then," Dana said. "My reaction to the newspaper story wasn't ladylike, it was childish, with a hefty dose of ridiculous hysterics thrown in. I want to apologize for my behavior, Kurt. I don't blame you for making certain that I wouldn't disappear in a cloud of dust. I'm very sorry for the way I acted."

"Oh." Kurt frowned slightly. "Well, I'm apologizing for treating you like a criminal under guard. I was way out of line, had no right to do that. I'm sorry, Dana. I even brought you a peace offering." He took the china kittens from his pocket. "Here. I found this out at Winona's place this morning, and I thought you might like it."

Dana cradled the figurine in both hands and held it up to eye level.

"It's wonderful," she said, smiling. "The white kitten looks just like Mouse. Thank you, Kurt. I'll treasure this, I really will."

"I'm glad you like it."

Kurt closed the distance between them and framed Dana's face in his hands.

"This has been a long day," he said. "I've had a knot the size of a bowling ball in my gut over the way we parted this morning. If we hadn't patched things up, I'd probably have an ulcer by tomorrow. I can't handle being at odds with you the way we were today, Dana.''

''I can't, either,'' she said softly.

''Well, we've apologized to each other, so there's only one thing left to do to erase the whole thing.''

''Which is?'' Dana asked.

''We kiss and make up.''

''I'll vote for that.''

And so Kurt kissed her.

The kiss was sweet and gentle, meant to soothe hurt feelings and ragged nerves, and it did, pushing the grim memories of their upset into oblivion.

Then the kiss intensified, rushing on, taking them into a place of heated desire and soaring passion. Their tongues met in the welcoming darkness of Dana's mouth, dueling, stroking, fanning the flames of want and need. Their hearts thundered, and their labored breathing echoed loudly in the small, quiet room.

Kurt finally lifted his head.

''Whoa,'' he said, his voice gritty. He drew a rough breath.

''Whoa?'' Dana said dreamily.

''Yes, for now we're set on whoa. Hold the thought, though. We have somewhere very important to go.''

''We do? Where?''

''My dear Ms. Bailey,'' he said, smiling, ''it's meat loaf night at the Hip Hop Café.''

The next three days were bliss.

Dana smiled so much she was amazed that her cheeks didn't ache.

Kimberly was delighted to take over the care of Mickey, Minnie and Mouse, and Dana and Kurt drove to Billings. They spent an entire day tromping from store to store, picking out new furniture for Kurt's house. They chose carpeting, as well, and arrangements were made for delivery to Whitehorn.

They ate dinner at a romantic restaurant, where a roving violinist serenaded them, then spent the night in a plush hotel, where they consumed a room-service breakfast while propped against the pillows on the enormous bed.

Upon their return to Whitehorn, they made several trips to Winona's Stop 'N' Swap to deposit Kurt's old furniture. Their purchases arrived, the carpeting was installed, and then they squabbled, laughing all the while, about the placement of the new furniture.

While the three days were sweet bliss, carefree and fun, the nights were pure ecstasy. They made exquisitely beautiful love over and over. Sated, contented, they slept, only to awaken and reach eagerly for each other.

What Dana did *not* do was think.

She didn't ask Kurt why he was suddenly free, not having to report into work.

She didn't dwell on Natalie or the nightmare her twin had created.

She didn't count down the dwindling number of days she had left to be with Kurt.

She simply savored each glorious moment shared, and tucked a multitude of wondrous memories away in the treasure chest in her heart.

* * *

Two days before the trial date, Judd contacted Kurt and asked him to come into the office. Kurt left Dana at the motel, where she planned to gather her clothes and head for the Laundromat with one of her trusty books in tow.

Kurt went to the police station and entered Judd's office.

"Sit," the sheriff said.

Kurt did as instructed and looked at Judd questioningly.

"The public defender for the perp who shot Clem," Judd said, "has filed a motion for a change of venue, claiming his client can't get a fair trial in Whitehorn. His petition also states that a judge in Billings should rule on the motion, because Judge Kate Randall Walker has known Clem for years."

"Ah, hell," Kurt said. "What a jerk."

"Kate has to comply," Judd said. "She's faxing the information to Billings and will ask for a quick ruling. However, the starting of the trial will definitely be delayed."

"Let me know what Dana says when you tell her," Kurt said dryly.

"Nice try, but you get to break the news to her."

"She's going to go ballistic, Judd." Kurt got to his feet. "Anything else?"

"No. It's been quiet around here."

"Have there been any more incidents at the Kincaid ranch?"

"Nope," Judd said, "but no one is relaxing out there. There hasn't been any pattern to the timing of those weird happenings, so they're all on edge. Rand said he was really grateful for the way J. D. Cade stays loose and cool, which helps the other hands hang in there."

"I like J. D. Cade," Kurt said, nodding. "He's steady, just steps in and does what needs to be done without showboating about it. Rand is lucky to have him on the payroll during this mess at the ranch."

"Yes, he is," Judd said. "So how are you and Dana getting on?"

"Fine."

"Have you found any answers to all those questions you had?"

"No."

"Am I correct in deducing that you don't wish to discuss this subject?"

"Yes."

"See ya, Kurt."

"See ya, Judd."

When Kurt left the building, he walked slowly along the sidewalk, deep in thought.

He was about to burst the really nice bubble he and Dana had been existing in during the past several days and sensational nights, he thought, and he was none too happy about it.

He slouched onto a wooden bench beneath a mulberry tree, stretched out his legs and scowled into space.

What would Dana do and say when he told her that the starting of the trial has been delayed? he wondered. She was going to be upset big-time, no doubt about it.

"You're definitely in trouble, Noble." Kurt planted his hands on his thighs and pushed himself to his feet. "It's called kill the messenger."

Chapter Twelve

Dana slipped a freshly laundered lightweight sweater onto a hanger, then walked toward the minuscule closet in the motel room.

"I see," she said, her back to Kurt. "And you actually have no idea how long this delay in the trial starting will be?"

Kurt watched Dana intently from where he sat at the small table.

"No," he said, "but Kate will request an immediate decision on the motion for a change of venue. Hopefully the judge in Billings will deny the petition right away, and we'll be back in action."

"Or it could take days, even weeks, to get a ruling on the motion." Dana hung up the sweater, then crossed the room to sit opposite Kurt at the table. "Right?"

"I suppose, but Kate is a highly respected judge in

these parts. I truly believe her request for expediency on the ruling will carry some weight.''

"Well, time will tell," Dana said, shrugging. "You *will* keep me fully informed?''

"Of course, but..." Kurt stopped speaking and shook his head. "I thought you'd holler the roof down.''

"None of this is your fault, Kurt," Dana said, massaging her temples with her fingertips. "I know all about the shenanigans that lawyers can pull, due to the fact that I'm an attorney myself.''

"I'm relieved that you're taking this so calmly, I really am." Kurt paused. "What's wrong? Do you have a headache?''

"Yes, I woke up with it this morning, and it just won't go away. My stomach is a bit upset, too. I think I might be catching the flu.''

"Maybe you just need something to eat," Kurt said, frowning. "Why don't we go to the Hip Hop and have some dinner?''

"I don't think I could eat anything. I feel sort of achy, and very tired. The best thing for me is a nice warm bath and a solid night's sleep. I'll be as good as new in the morning.''

"Are you sure?''

"Positive," she said, managing to produce a smile. "I can usually shake off the flu very quickly, if I get plenty of rest at the onset. It's just a bug, Kurt. I'll be fine tomorrow.''

Kurt got to his feet. "I hate to leave you alone if you're not up to par.''

"It's better if you do. You don't want to come down with the flu. I'm glad Kimberly still has the kittens. I won't have to get up in the night to feed them.''

Kurt smiled. ''She's fallen in love with the terrific trio. I don't believe we're going to be getting them back.'' His smile faded. ''Look, why don't you come home with me? That way, I'd be right there if you needed anything.''

''No, no, that's not necessary. I'm going to be dead to the world as soon as I've had my bath.''

''Well...''

Dana stood and smiled up at Kurt.

''I appreciate your willingness to play Florence Nightingale,'' she said, ''but I'll be dandy right here, snoozing away.''

''All right, but call me if you need something, or if you decide you'd better see a doctor, or...''

''Yes, Mr. Fussbudget, I will,'' Dana said, laughing. ''Now go, before I spread my germs.''

Kurt drew one thumb over Dana's lips, and she shivered at the simple, yet sensuous, foray.

''I'm going to miss having you next to me in bed tonight,'' Kurt said, looking directly into Dana's eyes. ''I've gotten used to your being there, and it's nice, very nice. I suppose you're going to say I shouldn't kiss you because you're contagious.''

''Absolutely.''

''You're a mean lady.'' Kurt kissed her gently on the forehead. ''Good night, Dana. Sleep well, and remember to call me if you need anything. I'll see you tomorrow morning.''

Dana nodded, then watched Kurt leave the room. As the door clicked closed quietly behind him, she jerked as though it had been a loud noise.

''Goodbye, Kurt,'' she whispered, willing herself

not to cry. "I'm sorry, but this is the last straw. *I can't stay here any longer.*"

Feeling as though her heart were breaking, Dana pulled her suitcase from the closet and began to pack.

She'd get ready to go, then wait the hour or so until it was dark, she thought. Then she'd drive away from Whitehorn, Montana, disappear into the night.

She'd never see Kurt Noble again.

The ache of unshed tears closed Dana's throat as she drew a steadying breath.

I will not cry, she vowed silently. All the pent-up tears waiting to flow that she'd refused to allow to spill forth from the beginning of this nightmare were threatening to consume her.

No. She had to maintain control. She mustn't cry, not yet. To weep would be her undoing, was a luxury she couldn't afford, not yet.

But, oh, God, she thought, stopping to stare at the doorway that Kurt had gone through, she hadn't even had the chance to kiss Kurt Noble goodbye.

Kurt entered his house, wandered into the kitchen, opened the refrigerator and looked at the offerings available for his dinner. He slammed the door closed again, then strode to his bedroom, where he changed into jeans and a navy blue sweatshirt.

Back in the living room, he slouched in one of the comfortable new chairs and stared into space.

Winona Cobbs, he thought, had told him to listen to the whispers from his heart to discover whether he was in love with Dana. Fine. He was all tuned in to receive any whispers his heart might transmit.

But right now?

The message he was receiving was from his gut, from instincts born of years of being a cop.

His brain was hammering at him, replaying the scene in Dana's motel room over and over. What had happened when he told her the trial had been postponed—her "Oh, well, what the hell?"—reaction wasn't ringing true.

And then Dana had announced suddenly that she thought she was coming down with the flu? She didn't want to eat dinner, or spend the night at his house? She just wanted to be left alone to sleep?

Dana wanted to be left alone.

Dana wanted to be left alone to...

Kurt lunged to his feet. "Leave town. Damn it to hell, Dana is going to skip."

Dana peered through the narrow opening in the faded drapes on the window of the motel room. Darkness had fallen, and millions of twinkling stars glowed in the black-velvet sky.

Lights shone in the motel office at the street end of the row of rooms, and a car was parked nearby. One other car was in front of the third room.

She shifted her perusal to the woods that butted against her room. The tall trees looked suddenly ominous, like towering sentinels on guard duty. A crisp breeze was blowing, causing the tops of the trees to weave and dip in the humanlike, eerie rhythm of a ritualistic dance.

Dana dropped the edge of the curtain and pressed both hands flat on her churning stomach.

There was nothing frightening out there, she told herself. Her imagination was playing nasty tricks on her because she was about to sneak out of Whitehorn like a thief in the night. All she had to do was walk through the doorway, put her suitcase in the car and drive away.

Taking a steadying breath, Dana walked to the bed to retrieve her purse and suitcase. Her hand stilled in midair as she reached for the strap of her purse, her gaze falling on the spread-covered pillows.

Vivid memories of the lovemaking shared with Kurt in that bed assaulted her, causing her cheeks to flush with warmth and her heart to quicken.

Oh, Kurt, she thought. She would miss him so much, so very much. The future seemed to be stretching before her like a bleak, empty highway that she was destined to travel alone.

Kurt would be so angry, so hurt, when he discovered that she was gone. He'd feel betrayed by her, no doubt viewing her as a lying, scheming woman who had toyed with his emotions, his caring, played games, then tossed him away like an object that no longer interested her, or served any purpose.

Dana pressed her fingertips to her lips, struggling yet again to keep threatening tears at bay. She leaned forward and smoothed the spread over the pillow where Kurt had laid his head, where Kurt had slept so peacefully after they journeyed to the place of the glorious wildflowers...together.

Oh, Dana, quit torturing yourself, she thought. *Just go. Get in your car, leave Whitehorn and don't look back. Whatever you do, don't look back.*

She snatched up her purse from the bed, slipped the strap over her shoulder, then grasped the handle of the suitcase.

At the door, she hesitated, remembering how threatening everything beyond that room had appeared when she peeked through the drapes. Squaring her shoulders and lifting her chin, she opened the door and stepped outside, closing the door behind her with a quiet click.

She glanced around quickly, suffused with fear, then hurried to the car. After unlocking the passenger side door, she placed her suitcase on the front seat, eased the door shut, then started toward the front of the car.

"Going somewhere?" a deep voice asked.

Kurt! Dana's mind screamed.

She stopped dead in her tracks and spun around in the direction of his voice. She gasped as Kurt moved out of the trees to stand in the glow of the yellow lightbulb mounted on the wall by her room.

"Kurt," Dana said, her voice trembling as badly as her knees.

"Yes, ma'am, that's me," he said, a rough, angry edge to his voice. "Detective Noble at your service, ma'am. And I repeat...are you going somewhere?" He started toward her, his furious gaze locked on her face, her eyes.

"I... What I mean is..." Dana took a step backward as Kurt closed the distance between them. She thudded against the car, halting her retreat, and wrapped her hands protectively around her elbows. "I was just..."

"Leaving Whitehorn?"

Kurt stopped directly in front of her.

His eyes, Dana thought frantically. Kurt's eyes were like cold chips of blue ice, and his pulse was beating wildly in his temple. He looked big, powerful and menacing, his fury a nearly palpable entity that she could touch as it crackled through the air.

A shiver coursed through Dana.

"You were spying on me," she said, striving for a bravado that remained beyond her reach. "How dare you treat me like a—"

"Liar?" Kurt said, interrupting her. "A phony? You sure did find a miraculous cure for your bout of the flu."

"I..."

"Give it a rest, Dana. You were cutting out, weren't you? Leaving Whitehorn. You don't give a rip about Clem, or testifying at the trial of the scum who shot that decent old man. Even more, you don't give a damn about me, us, what we have—no, correct that, what I *thought* we had together. None of it meant anything to you. You're a real piece of work, Dana Bailey, you really are."

"Kurt, please, listen to me. I know you're angry and hurt, but you just don't understand. I can't stay here any longer. Too much time had passed as it was, then the trial was delayed, and... I have to go. I have to find Natalie before..." Dana shook her head.

"Before what?" Kurt snapped. "Are you ready to tell me the whole story? Do you trust me enough yet?"

"Trust? You're talking about trust?" Dana said, nearly shrieking. "You, who was hiding in the trees, watching me, waiting to see if I'd stay put in my room like a good little girl? Where, pray tell, was your trust in me tonight, Kurt Noble?"

"Where was my trust? Listening to the voice of my instincts as a cop. It sure as hell wasn't hearing any of Winona's famous whisperings from the heart."

"What?"

"Forget it," Kurt said, slicing one hand through

the air. "Bottom line, Dana. Do you intend to tell me what is going on, or not?"

Dana shook her head. "No. I can't."

"You *won't*. By the way, you might be interested to know that Winona sensed danger surrounding you and Natalie. It could be directed at one of you, or both of you. She couldn't be certain, because you have the same face. I'm a cop, remember? Part of my job is to protect people, protect *you*."

"No, I don't want you involved in this."

Kurt muttered an earthy expletive, then stared up at the sky for a long moment in an attempt to gain control of his raging emotions. He let out a pent-up breath, then looked at Dana again.

"You just don't get it, do you?" he said quietly, his voice edged with weariness. "I *am* involved, Dana, because you're a very important part of my life. You can't pick and choose what you'll share with me, call all the shots as to how our relationship is set up. It just doesn't work that way."

"Relationship?" Dana said, blinking away sudden and unwelcome tears. "That word indicates something long-term, something that encompasses a future together. We don't have that, Kurt. We never did. We've known from the very beginning that I would be leaving Whitehorn."

"Things change. People change. When you met me, I was planning on returning to Seattle. Now I've made the decision to stay on here, settle in, think about what I want to have in my future."

"And you're free to do that," Dana said, flinging out her arms. "I'm not, don't you see? I'm caught up in the nightmare that Natalie created, and I don't have the luxury of planning anything beyond getting that horrible mess set to rights.''

"Ah, yes, the nightmare, the mess, the whatever-it-is that your naughty twin sister stirred up,'' Kurt said, his voice ringing with sarcasm. "The situation you refuse to share with me, allow me to become involved in.''

"Kurt...''

"Forget it. We're just retracking old ground, running in circles.'' He paused and frowned. "So what do I do with you now? The minute I turn my back, you're going to be long gone.''

"No, I won't,'' Dana said, sighing. "I'll stay and testify at the trial.''

"Yeah, right. Have you got a bridge you'd like to sell me, too?''

"I promise, Kurt,'' she said, splaying one hand on her heart. "I'm giving you my word of honor. Don't you trust me at all?''

"About as much as you trust me. That's not saying a whole hell of a lot, is it? Give me the keys to your car.''

"No. You're treating me like a prisoner again.''

"You leave me no choice. I'm going to stay as close to you as I possibly can. When I just can't be with you, your not having a car should slow you down enough until I'm back on duty, sticking to you like glue.''

"I just promised you that I wouldn't leave White-horn until I've testified at the trial,'' Dana said, her voice rising.

"Mmm,'' Kurt said, extending one hand palm up. "The keys.''

Dana smacked the keys into Kurt's hand, then spun

around and retrieved her suitcase from the car. She slammed the car door, deciding the action was a nice touch in letting Kurt know how angry she was. She marched to the door of the room and turned the knob.

"Drat," she said, her back to Kurt. "I left my key inside, and the door locked automatically."

"What a shame. Sort of blew your temper-tantrum exit, didn't it? You were going to flounce inside, then slam the door in my face."

She turned to face him, her eyes narrowed. "I do *not* flounce, Detective Noble. That indicates a dramatic and phony performance, the likes of which I do not indulge in. I'm very angry with you for not trusting my word, my promise."

"I'm not too crazy about you at the moment, either, lady. I'll go up to the office and get another key. I assume you'll be here when I get back?"

"You're stubborn and despicable."

"And you, Dana Bailey," Kurt said over his shoulder, as he started toward the motel office, "are exhausting."

The next morning, Kurt entered his office and sank into the chair behind his desk. He propped his elbows on the arms of the chair and made a steeple of his hands, tapping his fingers against his lips. A deep frown knit his brows as he stared at the telephone.

He was dead tired again, he thought. He'd stretched out fully clothed next to Dana on the bed in her motel room the previous night, and gotten only snatches of sleep.

The angry tension between them had seemed to hang in the air with an oppressive weight. No words had been spoken during the long, dark hours until dawn.

Stating brusquely that he'd be back later, he'd left Dana in the room, then driven home to shower, change clothes, eat breakfast and feed the damnable cats.

Now here he was, and it was decision time, he thought. He could choose to continue to wait, hoping that Dana would come to trust him enough to tell him exactly what Natalie had done.

Or he could investigate on his own, declare by his actions that he'd lost faith in Dana's caring for him, in her honesty, in the very essence of what they had together.

"Hell," he said, dragging both hands down his face.

Trust, Kurt thought. It was a small, five-letter word. It was an issue that was powerful enough to tear him and Dana apart.

He didn't care if she was hung up on a technicality as to whether or not they had a relationship. They did have one, damn it.

So, okay, the future was clouded by whatever trouble Dana was in, as well as a long list of unanswered questions regarding exactly what they might have together.

But in the now, in the moment at hand, they were lovers, were equal partners in a relationship. A relationship in which mutual trust was very, very shaky.

Danger, Kurt thought suddenly. Winona had sensed danger hovering over the Dana with two faces. With everything else that was piled on his beleaguered brain, he'd temporarily forgotten about the danger.

"That cooks it," he said aloud.

Kurt reached for the receiver to the telephone.

* * *

In the early afternoon, Dana trudged along the side of the road, a plastic bag filled with library books clutched to her chest with both arms.

This, she thought, had not been a great idea. Walking a couple of miles into town to exchange her novels and burn off some stress with the exercise seemed like a fine plan, until her arms began to ache from the weight of the books.

"Drat," she said aloud.

She'd been a picture-perfect prisoner, she mused on. She'd gotten a piece of tape from the manager on duty in the motel office and left a note on her door addressed to Kurt, telling him exactly where she was going and approximately what time she expected to return.

Kurt was so furious at her for attempting to leave town in the dead of night. She'd panicked, the delay of the start of the trial causing her to react without thinking things through.

Yes, she needed to leave Whitehorn as quickly as possible to help in the search for Natalie. Pete Parker's trip to Detroit had been a dead end. Natalie had been leaving a false trail. She'd reserved a room at a hotel with Dana's credit card, but Pete had spoken with the maid, who said the bed hadn't been slept in, or the towels used.

There had to be *something* she and Peter were missing—a clue, an idea, that would enable them to find Natalie. She needed to spend endless hours with the detective brainstorming, going over every detail of what they already knew.

But another part of her wanted to testify at the trial

here in Whitehorn, make certain that the man who had shot Clem paid the price for the horrendous crime.

Dana sighed as she continued her trek.

Kurt would never believe her if she told him she fully intended to be on that witness stand. She'd destroyed his trust in her by her sneaky deed of trying to leave town.

She'd run out of emotional energy as far as staying angry at Kurt for spying on her from the woods was concerned. The man was a trained detective, for crying out loud. Her instant case of the flu had obviously come across as phony as it actually had been, and Kurt had simply followed his fine-tuned instincts.

"I've messed up everything," Dana said aloud.

There would be no more precious memories to keep of the time left to share with Kurt if his anger didn't cool and his hurt diminish. He was like a statue carved from stone, with no warmth radiating from his blue eyes.

How could she chip away at the man of granite to reveal the true Kurt once again? How could she get him to trust and believe in her once more, to know that she would stay in Whitehorn to testify at the trial?

The only thing that might give her back her Kurt was to tell him the whole story of what Natalie had done. Tell him the complete truth. But she just couldn't, wouldn't, do that.

The beep of a horn brought Dana from her troubled thoughts, and she looked over to see a pickup truck stopped in the road.

"Ms. Bailey?" a man said. "J. D. Cade. We met at the library a while back."

"Oh, yes," Dana said, halting her step and smiling. "I remember. How are you, J.D.?"

"Fine. Where are you headed?"

"To the library."

"Would you like a lift, Ms. Bailey? I know your mother probably taught you not to accept rides from strangers, but we've been properly introduced."

"Call me Dana, and I'd be grateful for a ride. These books are getting heavier by the minute."

Settled in the cab of the truck with a tail-wagging Freeway between them, Dana thanked J.D. again for rescuing her from her it-was-a-crummy-idea walk into town.

"No problem," J.D. said, smiling. "It's nice to have company. Freeway isn't big on conversation."

"What kind of dog is he?" Dana said, frowning slightly at the furry creature.

J.D. shrugged. "Beats me. That's a mystery never to be solved."

"What about the mystery of those strange happenings out at the ranch where you work? Do you think you'll solve that?"

"We'd better. We can't keep hands on the payroll for long, because they get spooked, come to believe the spread is haunted by ghosts, or spirits, or some such thing. Believe me, it's very frustrating to have these episodes taking place right under our noses and not be able to catch anyone in the act."

"What do they hope to accomplish by this nonsense?" Dana said.

"I don't know. Shut down the Kincaid ranch? But why? It's owned by a three-year-old angel named Jennifer. Man, that is one cute little girl."

"Well, no one could have a grudge against a three-year-old baby,'' Dana said. ''The whole thing doesn't make any sense.''

''Tell me about it,'' J.D. said. ''The tension out at the ranch gets worse every day. It's a lot for the foreman, Rand Harding, to deal with.'' He paused. ''There's the library, just up ahead.''

''I appreciate the taxi service.''

Just as J.D. parked in front of the library, Judd Hensley and Travis Bains came down the sidewalk together. Judd introduced Travis to Dana as the quartet stood on the sidewalk.

''You have no idea how much I've been looking forward to meeting you,'' Travis said to Dana.

''Oh, well, thank you,'' Dana said, rather surprised at Travis's gushy words.

''Kurt and I grew up together,'' Travis said. ''We're still best friends.''

''Oh, I see,'' Dana said, smiling. ''Then you must be pleased that he has decided to stay on in Whitehorn permanently.''

''Everyone is tickled about it,'' Travis said. ''Kurt is a good man. The best. Top of the line.''

''What are you, Travis?'' Judd said. ''Kurt Noble's public relations director?''

''I'm just chatting,'' Travis said, grinning.

''Whatever,'' Judd said. ''How's it going at the ranch, J.D.?''

''The same,'' J.D. said. ''The men are tense and edgy, and Rand is trying to hold things together. I'm making a quick trip into town to get a toy, or book, for Jennifer. She's down with a cold.''

''Yeah, I heard,'' Judd said. ''My wife was talking to Jessica McCallum. Baby Jennifer has apparently been under the weather a lot lately.''

"All little kids get sick from time to time," Travis said. "J.D., just what is that thing in the cab of your truck?"

"Shh," Dana said, smiling. "Freeway is very sensitive about his looks. He wants to be appreciated for his heart of gold."

The four laughed, enjoying a carefree moment on a warm, sunny Montana afternoon in early June.

Kurt left the Hip Hop Café after having a late lunch and started down the sidewalk to return to the police station. The sound of laughter reached him, and he registered the thought that he envied anyone who was in such a chipper mood. As he walked farther, he saw the foursome who were so thoroughly enjoying themselves.

That was Dana, he thought incredulously. Dana Bailey was surrounded by J. D. Cade, Judd and Travis, and a good time was being had by all. Dana looked like a queen bee being paid homage by her loyal and fawning subjects.

How had Dana gotten into town? And what did she have to be so all-fired happy about? She obviously wasn't broken up over the fact that the two of them weren't even on speaking terms at the moment.

Travis and Judd were married men, but J. D. Cade was not. Yeah, sure, he'd liked what he saw of J.D. so far, but for all he knew, Cade was a randy cowboy on the prowl.

Kurt quickened his step.

J. D. Cade had better prowl somewhere else, he thought, because, by damn, Dana Bailey was Kurt Noble's lady!

Chapter Thirteen

Before Kurt could reach the group he was striding toward, they dispersed. Judd and Travis started across the street, J.D. got into his truck and turned the key in the ignition, and Dana began to stroll up the sidewalk leading to the library.

"Dana," Kurt yelled, "hold up!"

Dana stopped and turned as Kurt sprinted toward her, a deep scowl on his face.

Uh-oh, she thought. She felt like a mouse who had escaped from its cage and had just gotten caught. Detective Noble was obviously not a happy man.

Kurt stopped in front of Dana and planted his hands on his hips.

"What are you doing here?" he said gruffly. "How did you get into town? Do you enjoy being surrounded by panting men?"

"Well, now, let's see here," Dana said pleasantly,

tapping one fingertip against her chin. "I'm returning library books. I was walking, then J.D. gave me a ride. Judd, Travis and J.D. weren't panting, they were laughing, and, yes, I enjoyed their cheerful company."

"Mmm," Kurt said.

Dana raised her eyebrows. "Anything else? Oh, I left a note on my door at the motel informing you as to exactly where I was."

"Oh." Kurt ran one hand over the back of his neck. "You accepted a ride from J. D. Cade? Did he make a move on you?"

"He was a perfect gentleman, and you are beginning to sound like a jealous lover, which isn't very becoming."

"I sound like a jealous…" Kurt paused. "You're right, I do. Classy, huh? Maturity to the maximum."

"About as classy and mature as my panic-driven attempt to leave town in the middle of the night," Dana said. "I do believe we're even."

"What about the issue of trust?" Kurt said quietly.

Dana sighed. "Can't we just leave that alone, Kurt? I don't want to be fighting with you during the time we have left together. I'm sorry I tried to leave Whitehorn. You're sorry you just acted like a jealous jerk."

"Well, I will have to stay very close to you," he said, a slow smile beginning to creep across his face. "You know, in case you get another one of those panic attacks and decide to split."

"Good idea," Dana said, matching his smile.

"So here we are again, having mended fences. All that's left to do is kiss and make up."

"In the middle of downtown Whitehorn? Bad plan. Everyone will know that Kurt Noble kissed Dana Bailey on the sidewalk leading to the library. Tongues will wag. Gossip will buzz through the air like busy bees.''

''Guaranteed, because Lily Mae Wheeler is coming this way. She's a better broadcaster than the six o'clock news on television.''

''And you still intend to kiss me?'' Dana said.

''Absolutely,'' Kurt said, grinning. ''That will deliver my message to J. D. Cade, and any other guy who might be offering you rides in their trucks, or whatever.''

Dana laughed. ''You're terrible.''

''No,'' Kurt said, framing her face in his hands, ''I'm just protecting what's mine.''

Then he lowered his head and kissed her.

Mine, Dana's mind hummed, as she savored the taste and feel of Kurt's lips on hers. She was his. He was hers. They were together. Yes.

Kurt raised his head slowly, reluctantly.

''I think I'd better stop kissing you now,'' he said, his voice slightly gritty, ''before I give Lily Mae more of a show than I intended.'' He took a step backward. ''There goes Lily Mae, hustling into the Hip Hop like her britches were on fire.''

''I repeat,'' Dana said, smiling, ''you're terrible.''

''Do you mind that the whole town knows we're involved with each other, having a relationship, an affair, a tryst, a—?''

''Enough.'' Dana laughed and shook her head. ''No, I don't mind, but you're the one who is going to live here after I…'' Her smile faded. ''Erase that. Let's just enjoy the time we have.''

''Yeah, well…'' Kurt sighed. ''Okay, look, you go do your thing at the library, then come over to the police station. We'll cook dinner out at my place tonight, all right?''

''Perfect.''

Kurt dropped a quick kiss on Dana's lips.

''See ya.''

''Bye, Kurt.''

Dana watched Kurt as he strode away. She simply stood there and drank in the sight of his masculine, loose-hipped way of walking, his broad shoulders and powerful legs.

Mine, she mentally repeated. *For now, Kurt Noble is mine and, oh, heavens, that's a glorious feeling.*

Kurt was smiling when he entered the police station, and he had a definite spring in his step.

''What are they serving at the Hip Hop today, Kurt?'' a uniformed officer said. ''Happy gas?''

''I'll never tell,'' Kurt said, not breaking stride, ''but Lily Mae will.''

He went into his office, sat down in his chair and picked up a pink message slip that Kimberly had placed in the center of his desk. As he read what Kim had written, a cold chill replaced the warmth that had consumed him.

Kurt sank back in the chair and stared at the paper. He was to call Detective Bonner of the Chicago police force, who was returning Kurt's telephone inquiry.

Kurt let out a pent-up breath and stared at the ceiling for a long moment, before looking at the pink slip again.

This was it, he thought. Truth time. Lord, he wished he had a magic wand, could place the words he wanted to hear in Detective Bonner's mouth before the cop spoke.

He'd have Bonner say that Dana Bailey had skipped on a badly overdrawn checking account and several maxed-out credit cards. No big deal, but enough for the authorities to want to find her and slap her with a fine.

Kurt nodded.

Yeah, that was the nightmare Natalie had created. She'd used Dana's checks and credit cards and the cops thought Dana was the guilty party. Messy, but fixable. End of story.

"Hear me thinking, Bonner," Kurt said, under his breath. "Don't blow your lines."

Fifteen minutes later, Kurt's shoulder throbbed with a steady pain from his having tensed every muscle in his body. A cold knot twisted in his gut and his knuckles were white from his tight hold on the telephone receiver.

"Yeah, it is big-time," he said. "Selling insider trading information is the yuppie crime of the decade that gets people a nice stretch in the slam....

"Dana Bailey? No, she's...she's long gone. She came through Whitehorn several weeks ago and... I don't know, she acted edgy, nervous. I couldn't get her off of my mind, so I thought I'd check her out, since I'd noticed her Illinois license plate. I started with you guys in Chicago....

"Nope, sorry, I don't have a clue as to where she was headed.... Sure, I'll keep my eyes open, but I doubt she'd double back through here. We're just a dot on the map.... You bet. Thanks, and good luck, Bonner."

Kurt replaced the receiver with a visibly shaking hand, then leaned his head back on the top of the chair and closed his eyes.

Ah, Dana, his mind screamed, no! It was a sick rerun of what had happened in Seattle, déjà vu in its cruelest form.

Kurt opened his eyes and lunged forward, hitting the desk with one fist and causing a white-hot pain to shoot up his arm and sear his damaged shoulder.

God, what a fool he'd been...again, he fumed. He'd fallen for Dana's phony spiel about her twin sister having created the famous nightmare Dana was caught up in. For all he knew, Dana didn't even have a twin. Even if there was a sister named Natalie, it didn't make sense that she would have had ready access to the information Dana had illegally sold.

Dana Bailey was guilty as sin.

And he'd fallen for her sob story, hook, line and sinker. He'd been suckered in by big blue eyes and womanly arms beckoning to him to come to her, make love to her, declare her to be his lady.

No wonder Dana had been shook up when her whereabouts was revealed in that Billings newspaper story. The Chicago cops were combing the country for her.

But Ms. Bailey was a sharp cookie. Hooking up with a cop in Whitehorn had given her an inside track as far as knowing whether Judd Hensley had been contacted about Dana Bailey, fugitive from the law, was concerned.

Kurt sighed. It was a weary-sounding sigh that seemed to come from the very depths of his soul.

It had all been a calculated plan to Dana, a means to an end. She didn't give a rip about him as a man, a major player in her life. He was nothing more than a potential source of information as to whether or not the cops had picked up her trail.

"Damn it," Kurt said, getting to his feet.

He stared at the telephone, his eyes narrowed.

Why hadn't he told Detective Bonner that Dana Bailey was in Whitehorn, Montana? Why hadn't he turned her in, agreed to keep her in custody in jail until Bonner could fly in and take her back to Chicago? He'd had the opportunity to blow the whistle on Dana, but he hadn't done it. Why?

Kurt nodded.

He knew why. He wanted a chance to confront Dana with her tower of lies. The last time he allowed his emotions to dictate his actions, he'd ended up with a bullet in his shoulder as he lay unconscious on the floor in a pool of his own blood.

This time, by damn, he was going to square off against the woman who had used him for her own selfish purposes. He would have closure, the last word, the means to shut the emotional door and walk away.

Maybe, just maybe, the pain of Dana's betrayal wouldn't last forever, wouldn't haunt him into infinity.

Kurt strode out of his office, told Kimberly he was done for the day, then left the police station. When he arrived on the sidewalk, he saw Dana approaching.

Each step she took to close the distance between them seemed to strike him like a physical blow.

That wasn't Dana coming to meet him. It wasn't *his* Dana, who had brought sunshine and laughter into his life, helped change his shabby house into a warm and welcoming home, who had traveled with him to burst upon the wondrous wildflowers when they made love.

The woman who had just waved and quickened her step was a stranger. A liar. A criminal on the run from the law. A user. A person who had toyed with his emotions, played with him as if he were a marionette, jumping as she jerked the strings.

She wasn't remotely close to who he had believed her to be.

And, Lord, that hurt.

"Hi, hi, hi," Dana called.

She ran the last twenty feet separating them and stopped in front of Kurt, a smile on her face, her blue eyes sparkling.

"Look what I found at that little gift shop down the street," she said, pulling an object from a sack. "It's a tiny shadow box that will be perfect for the figurine of the kittens that you gave me. I'm so tickled with it. Isn't it pretty?"

"Mmm," Kurt said.

"In my purse is a gigantic novel I checked out of the library, too. It ought to keep me out of trouble."

"It's a bit late for that thought, isn't it?" Kurt said, a rough edge to his voice.

Dana frowned. "What on earth is wrong, Kurt? You've certainly changed moods since we parted in front of the library."

"That was a lifetime ago. Come on, let's go to the motel. You and I are going to have a chat."

"But..."

"Now, Dana."

Kurt turned and started toward where his vehicle was parked. Dana followed, totally confused.

* * *

In Dana's room at the motel, she sat down on the edge of the bed and looked at Kurt questioningly. He grabbed one of the chairs by the table and set it about three feet in front of her. Straddling it backward, he layered his arms on the top of the back.

Cold, Dana thought, feeling a whisper of panic rush through her. Kurt's eyes were cold again, blue chips of ice. He was tense, appearing like a powerful animal about to leap forward to snare its prey.

Dear heaven, what had happened since they kissed on the sidewalk leading to the library? Kissed with Lily Mae Wheeler as a witness, so that all of Whitehorn would know that Dana Bailey and Kurt Noble were well and truly together, a romantically involved couple.

"Kurt?" Dana said tentatively.

Kurt rested his forehead on his arms for a moment as he drew a deep breath, letting it out slowly as he raised his head to look directly into Dana's eyes.

"Chicago cops." Kurt laughed, the sound a harsh bark. "There you go. It would make a great title for a television series. But the cop from Chicago who I talked to was very real, which is more than I can say for you."

Dana felt the color drain from her face. She clasped her trembling hands tightly in her lap.

"You're a perp," Kurt said. "How about that? The heroine of the convenience-store robbery is actually a fugitive running from the law. You sold insider trading information, and you're facing a jail sentence. Everything you've said and done since arriving in Whitehorn has been a lie, a bold-faced lie."

"No," Dana whispered. "No, that's not true."

"Just what *is* true?" Kurt said. "Do you even

know anymore? How do you keep all the lies straight, not trip yourself up?''

Kurt paused and shook his head.

''You must have laughed yourself silly over how easy I was to sucker in,'' he went on. ''The last woman who did a routine on me was the cause of my being shot. This time? I've discovered the truth while you were still playing your phony role. I'm one step ahead of you, and I hold all the cards.''

''Kurt, stop it, please,'' Dana said. ''Let me explain. Let me tell you the whole story, the complete truth about what happened in Chicago.''

''And *involve* me in your terrible nightmare? No thanks. Your offer is too little, too late.''

''I am *not* guilty of the charges against me, Kurt. I didn't sell that information. It was Natalie.''

''Yeah, right.'' Kurt pushed himself off the chair and stood, dragging a restless hand through his hair. ''Your twin sister just happened to know about the corporate merger, plus how to access your computer and print out the material. Give me a break, Dana.''

''She *did* know,'' Dana said, getting to her feet. ''Natalie showed up at my apartment after months of my not even knowing where she was. She said she'd changed, matured, wanted us to be truly sisters, friends.

''We hadn't been close, had nothing in common since we were very young children. I was thrilled to think I might actually have a sister again, a family.''

Dana sank back onto the bed, shaking her head.

''It was all part of a master plan that Natalie had put together. Well, it might have been someone else's brainstorm, and they paid her for her part in it. I just really don't know.''

Kurt folded his arms over his chest as he listened to Dana, no readable expression on his face.

"Natalie was staying with me at my apartment. She seemed so sincere in her desire for us to be close, have a bond, but looking back, I realize I wanted it to happen so much that I was vulnerable and very gullible."

"There's a lot of that going around," Kurt said gruffly.

"Oh, Kurt, I..."

"Forget it. Go on with your story."

Dana sighed. "What's the point? You don't believe a word I'm saying."

"I deserve to hear this fairy tale. I've paid my dues, don't you think? You decided from the beginning that I wasn't to become involved in your personal problems. I waited, Dana, waited and hoped you'd learn to trust me enough to share it all with me.

"It was because of what Winona said about sensing danger hovering around you, Natalie, whoever, that I decided I couldn't wait any longer. I called the Chicago police, and surprise, surprise, Dana Bailey is a felon on the lam, with an outstanding warrant for her arrest."

"Which is why I have to find Natalie, don't you see?" Dana said, her voice rising. "The police don't believe my story. No one does." Her voice dropped to a whisper. "Not even you."

Ah, man, Kurt thought, look at her. Dana's face was white as a sheet, her eyes were wide and pleading. She looked so lost, so alone and frightened. He wanted to take her into his arms, hold her close, promise her he'd do everything possible to find her sister. He'd stay by her side, comfort and protect her, until this whole crummy mess was cleared up. He'd...

Damn it, Noble, knock it off.

It was happening again. He was falling prey to the powerful, inexplicable attraction he felt to her, to those incredible big blue eyes, his own raging and confusing emotions.

No. No way. Not this time. Not again.

"You were saying that Natalie knew how to access your computer," he said, his voice flat and cold.

"Do you even believe there is a Natalie?"

"Yeah. It's too easy to check to determine if you have a twin sister. I can't imagine you being dumb enough to invent Natalie. So? Natalie and your computer?"

"Natalie asked me if she could go to work with me one day," Dana said, sounding thoroughly exhausted. "She'd decided the time had come to go back to school and get some marketable skills. She wanted to see if she was intimidated being in an office...and by computers...so I showed her how mine worked."

"Cripe," Kurt said, shaking his head.

"I know. It was a stupid thing to do. I even explained that there was a highly confidential file on the computer that was accessible only by a special code, which I proceeded to demonstrate for her."

Kurt muttered an earthy expletive.

"On the night Natalie impersonated me," Dana said, "I was sick in bed with a cold. She said she'd go to the store and buy me some juice. I never saw her again. She dressed in my clothes, went to my office and used my computer and printer to obtain the documents regarding the top-secret corporate merger.

"They have it all on a video from a security camera. There I am, just as bold as you please. Only it wasn't me, it was Natalie. They've arrested the man she sold the information to. He didn't think up the plan, it was presented to him."

"By Natalie?"

"Yes. What I don't know is if Natalie concocted the whole scheme on her own, or if there is someone else involved."

"Is Natalie intelligent enough to have done this alone?"

"I don't know, Kurt. I hardly know her."

"Mmm."

"So? What are you going to do? Call the police in Chicago and tell them I'm here? I assume, for whatever reasons you have, you didn't do that when you spoke to them earlier."

"No, I didn't. I want you to testify at the trial here. Clem deserves to have that perp put away."

"Oh," Dana said softly. "You kept silent for Clem's sake. You don't believe me, do you?"

Kurt hooked one hand on the back of his neck.

"I don't know what to believe right now, Dana. I've been blindsided by all this, need some time to sort through it all in my mind."

"I understand."

"This is worse than a bad movie," Kurt said, shaking his head. "Good twin. Bad twin. It's a pretty farfetched story."

"It's a true story."

"Maybe, maybe not. Well, reality check. It's time for dinner. I'm no longer in the mood to cook a meal together at my place. We'll grab a sandwich at the Hip Hop."

"I'm not hungry."

"You have to eat. Let's go."

"No."

"Dana, don't push me. You're going to feel very ridiculous if I carry you into the Hip Hop slung over my shoulder."

"You wouldn't dare."

"Try me."

"You're being despicable again, Detective Noble, which is something you seem to do on a regular basis." Dana stood and picked up her purse. "I'm going to order the most expensive thing on the menu, and you can pay the bill."

"Go for it."

Dana glared at him, then marched to the door. Kurt was right behind her. They stepped outside, into the cool summer evening. Darkness was falling, with just the traces of a disappearing sunset on the horizon.

"We'll go in my vehicle," Kurt said, "then decide later where we're spending the night. I'm not letting you out of my sight. I'm—"

In the next instant, a shot rang out, and a bullet slammed into the wall of the motel, missing Dana's head by only inches.

Kurt launched himself at Dana, rolling at the same time, so that her weight was on top of him as they hit the gravel parking lot next to his vehicle. A moan escaped from his lips as pain rocketed throughout his entire body from the impact to his injured shoulder. He shifted Dana off him and drew his gun.

"Oh, God," Dana said, her voice trembling.

"Shh," Kurt said, in a hushed voice. "Stay down. Don't move, or make a sound." He looked back at the hole in the wall. "The shot came from the woods.

The line of fire is blocked by my truck. Don't move. Understand?''

Dana nodded, her eyes wide and terrified.

Kurt crept to the end of the Blazer and took a quick glance at the woods.

"I'm going to fire my gun," he whispered to Dana.

He aimed above the trees, fired, then ducked back out of sight. He waited.... Three seconds passed, ten, then fifteen.

"That's it for today, folks," he said finally. "He probably split, because he thinks the guy in the office will have called the cops by now. That isn't true, because people hunt rabbits in that woods all the time."

"Kurt?" Dana said, hardly able to speak clearly. "Was he trying to kill me? Dear God, was he actually trying to kill me?"

Kurt stood, reholstered his gun, then helped Dana to her feet. He wrapped his arms around her and pulled her close.

"It sure seems that way," he said, tightening his hold as he felt her trembling. "Hey, look at the bright side."

"Which is?" she said, encircling his waist with her arms for support.

"I now believe every word of what you told me. I also now know that the danger Winona sensed is directed at you. But, Dana? I swear that nothing is going to happen to you. *Nothing.*"

Chapter Fourteen

They had to kill Dana.

That chilling thought plagued Kurt through the long, dark hours of the night, while an exhausted Dana slept close to his side in Kurt's bed.

Badly shaken by the events at the motel, Dana hadn't argued, had hardly spoken, when Kurt said they'd buy fast food for dinner and head for his place.

He'd treated her gently, carefully, knowing she was in a state of semishock from nearly being killed by an assassin's bullet. It was not a run-of-the-mill experience for a corporate attorney to have gone through.

Kurt sat on the front steps of the porch, a flannel shirt hanging unbuttoned and free of his jeans. He sipped coffee from a mug as the cats finished their breakfast and began to snooze in patches of sunlight.

He'd left Dana sleeping soundly in his bed, one hand tucked beneath her cheek like a child.

But Dana was a woman, Kurt thought. A woman who was in deep trouble. A woman who was, indeed, caught up in a living nightmare.

He swept his gaze over the lush countryside and inhaled the aromas of wildflowers and crisp, fresh air. The sky was changing from the gray of dawn to a brilliant blue, with puffs of white clouds dotting the heavens.

He needed this peaceful interlude, he knew, this moment of solitude, to gain a modicum of inner peace, tranquillity, a sense of control. Events were rushing forward like a raging river. He had to stop, take a cleansing breath, then he prepared to do what must be done.

He took another sip of the hot coffee, and with the warmth of the liquid came an emotional warmth, as well, a soothing, calming touch from an unseen hand.

Dana, his mind echoed. He'd nearly lost her. The bullet that slammed into the wall at the motel had missed her by mere inches. In a tick of time, a heartbeat, he'd almost had the woman he loved torn from his life forever.

Kurt stiffened, nearly spilling the coffee.

The woman he loved?

''Well,'' he said aloud, relaxing again as a smile crept onto his lips, ''now I know what whispers from the heart sound like.''

He was in love with Dana Bailey.

It all made sense, now that he'd taken a quiet moment to examine it. The pain he'd felt when he thought Dana had used him for her own purposes was born of a love thought to be betrayed.

The icy fear, accompanied by hot, raging anger, when Dana had almost been killed was the emotion of a man who had been a breath away from losing the woman he loved.

Dana.

Big blue eyes and swinging, silky blond hair, lush breasts and sweet, sweet lips. A quick wit and a feisty temper. A gentle side that cradled newborn kittens in the palm of her hand. Dana covered in paint, wearing only a skimpy, faded towel, standing naked and so glorious before him.

She was everything he'd ever dreamed of finding in his life's partner, his wife—and more. And he loved her with every breath in his body.

Kurt looked heavenward. "So be it," he said quietly, lifting his mug in acknowledgment.

He drained the mug, then reluctantly pulled his thoughts from the serene and awesome place of love just discovered to return to reality, the now and the danger.

Kurt set the mug on the porch, propped his elbows on his knees and steepled his hands, tapping his fingertips against his lips.

Natalie was mixed up with the big boys, he thought, frowning. The kind of scum who had hired guns at their beck and call.

The poor jerk who had been told to buy the corporate stock and had gotten himself arrested was a pawn, a false front. He would have been eliminated once the dust settled.

The high rollers were mad as hell because their carefully concocted plan had gone down the tubes. Now they were cleaning house, tying up loose ends, making certain there were no bread crumbs on the trail to lead back to them.

They had to kill Dana.

If Dana yelled loud enough and long enough that she was innocent, was the victim of an intricate plot involving her twin sister impersonating her, someone would listen. A good cop like Detective Bonner would finally sit up and pay attention.

With Dana out of the picture, the trail ended with the mysterious death of the guilty party. Natalie could reappear as the grieving twin of the sister who had broken the law, and stake a claim to all of Dana's possessions, as the only living relative of the dead felon.

Kurt nodded.

That was how it was set up. That was the only scenario that made any sense.

They had to kill Dana.

And Kurt Noble was willing to put his life on the line to make certain that didn't happen.

Because he was in love with Dana Bailey.

With a decisive nod, Kurt pushed himself to his feet, stepped over several sleeping felines and entered the house.

Early that afternoon, Kurt replaced the receiver to the telephone, then looked over at Dana, where she sat on the end of the sofa in his living room, her feet tucked up beside her.

"Okay," he said. "Pete Parker will be here to-morrow. He'll fly into Billings, rent a car and drive to Whitehorn. He's bringing everything he has in his file on Natalie. We'll go over it together, piece by piece."

"Kurt," Dana said, "there's something troubling me."

"What is it?"

"You're harboring a felon who has a warrant for her arrest hanging over her head. Your job, your entire career, is at stake. You're an officer of the law. If Judd knew that you…"

"Whoa." Kurt crossed the room and sat down beside Dana. "Judd *doesn't* know. I'm not telling him what's going on because I'd bet a buck he'd go along with what I'm doing. But it's harder for him to bend the rules. He's the boss. I don't want to put him in that position. As for me? Don't worry about it."

"Isn't Judd wondering why you haven't reported into work?"

"Nope. I'm officially unofficially sticking close to you to be certain you'll be in Whitehorn to testify at the trial. Hey, it's all going to work out just fine."

"How do you know that? What if we just can't find Natalie?"

"We'll find her. She may be involved with the pros, but she's still an amateur. She'll make a mistake." Kurt drew one thumb over Dana's cheek. "Trust me."

Dana smiled. "I do. I do trust you."

"And I trust you. That ingredient was a long time coming, but it's finally in place."

"Yes."

"So, okay, back to business. Let me ask you something. When Natalie showed up at your apartment unannounced, then moved in with you, did she seem impressed with your possessions? You know, where you lived, the furniture, your car, whatever?"

"Very much so," Dana said, nodding. "Everything

she owned was in a small duffel bag and her clothes were faded and out of style. She helped herself to my wardrobe from day one. She kept remarking on how much she liked my stereo system, the collection of CDs, my books, everything. She kept touching things, smiling and touching.''

Kurt nodded. ''Good. She was taking inventory of what would be hers when you went to jail. Now the plan is such that she'll inherit it all because...well...''

Dana shivered. ''Because they're hoping to kill me.''

''No, that isn't going to happen.''

''My God, my own sister is going happily along with a plan to murder me. How can she do such a terrible thing, Kurt?''

Kurt shifted Dana's legs to that he could sit closer to her. He encircled her shoulders with one arm and pulled her close, dropping a kiss on the top of her head.

''Listen to me,'' he said quietly. ''When my father split when I was a kid, I kept telling myself he'd come back. He wouldn't walk away from his son and daughter and never return. No way. I mean, hell, what kind of father would do such a thing?

''I watched for him for days, then weeks that turned into months. I finally had to accept the fact that he wasn't coming back. The hardest part, Dana, was that I didn't know why.''

''Oh, Kurt, I'm so sorry.''

''The point of this story is that in this thing called life there are some questions that never get answered. Don't drive yourself nuts, torment yourself, asking why Natalie is doing this to you. Accept the fact that

she *is* doing it, and find a place to put it. Understand?''

''Yes. Yes, I do. Thank you, Kurt. What you just
shared with me helped a great deal.''

What he'd shared? Kurt's mind echoed. What he
wanted to share with Dana was the rest of his life.
Later, Noble. This was not the time to declare his love
for Dana, ask her to marry him. She had enough on
her emotional plate to deal with. Once this mess was
behind them, though, he'd...

''Kurt?'' Dana said, bringing him from his
thoughts.

''Hmm?''

''Why did you ask me if Natalie was impressed by
my possessions?''

''It's a hunch and a hope. I'd like to get Pete Parker's input on it, but I'm thinking that Natalie just
might get antsy, want to gloat over her new worldly
goods. I want her to go to your apartment.''

''But the police are probably watching my place.''

''For *Dana* Bailey to show up. Natalie would go
as herself. The cops don't want her, but we do.''

Dana sighed and pressed her fingertips to her temples. ''A nightmare. It's all an awful, unbelievable
nightmare.''

''Yes, it is, but you're not alone anymore. Remember that, okay? I'm right here with you, and we'll see
this through to its proper end together. Together,
Dana.''

''Yes, and I'm so grateful for that, for you. Thank
you, Kurt.'' Dana paused. ''Could we go for a walk,
stroll through those pretty wildflowers beyond the
house?''

Kurt frowned. "No. It's too open in that area, with enough trees edging it to give someone cover."

"Dear heaven, do you believe they're out there right now, waiting, watching for an opportunity to shoot me?"

"I don't know, but we're playing this very safe, close to the cuff. Stay inside the house, and away from the windows."

"I hate this, Kurt."

"With just cause. It will all be over soon. I'm going to have a soda. Want one?"

"No thanks."

Dana watched as Kurt crossed the living room and disappeared into the kitchen, his words echoing in her mind.

It will all be over soon.

All and everything, she thought. The nightmare created by Natalie would end. The trial would be held, and she would testify, seek justice for Clem. She'd leave Whitehorn, Montana, return to Chicago and the life she led there. She'd never see Kurt Noble again.

It would all be over soon.

But not the ache in her heart for Kurt. Not the empty days and long, lonely nights without him. Not the fanciful images in her mind of standing by Kurt's side as they watched their children romp in the wild-flowers beyond their home.

For Dana knew that, despite the turmoil and upset, the unknowns about the future due to Natalie's actions, the fear, the horror of realizing there were people out there who wanted her dead, despite it all, her heart had been stronger than the oppression.

Her heart had soared above the darkness and danger. Her heart sang the ageless song of lovers.

Because, oh, yes, she was deeply and irrevocably in love with Kurt Noble.

But he would never know the depths of her feelings for him.

What was the point of telling him? she thought dismally. If, when, her innocence was proved, she'd return to her world, while Kurt remained in Whitehorn. There was no call for a corporate attorney in this tiny Montana town. Her career demanded that she live in a big city.

Oh, Dana, stop it, she admonished herself. She was mentally babbling. Just because she'd admitted to herself that she'd fallen in love with Kurt, that certainly didn't mean that *he* was in love with *her.*

She'd do well to stay firmly grounded in reality. They had to find Natalie. And, as incredible as it was, she, Dana Bailey, had to stay in the house, away from the windows, so that she wouldn't be killed by a bullet fired from a gun held in the hand of an enemy beyond those walls.

"I really, really hate this," she said, then drew a steadying breath.

A little after ten o'clock that night, Dana emerged from the bathroom in her nightshirt, then decided she wanted a glass of milk.

When she entered the living room, she was surprised to see that Kurt was talking on the telephone. She stopped and wrapped her hands around her elbows as she listened to his side of the conversation.

"I knew it," Kurt said into the receiver. He punched one fist in the air. "That's exactly how I had

Natalie pegged.... Absolutely. You stay put and watch that apartment like a hawk, Pete. She's going to jump the gun, no doubt about it.... Yeah, I realize she's home free if she appears as Natalie, but don't lose her, whatever you do....

"There has to be something in this mess that we're missing, that will prove that Natalie impersonated Dana.... Oh, I agree with you. The big boys can't be happy that Natalie is prancing around while there's unfinished business like Dana still breathing. They don't take kindly to the left hand not following the right hand's orders. Right. Keep in touch, step by step.... Yep. See ya, Pete."

Kurt hung up the receiver, then got to his feet, smiling when he saw Dana.

"That was your sharp detective, Ms. Bailey. Natalie used your charge card to buy a fancy bracelet in one store in Chicago, and a slew of clothes in another. She's not being a patient person, as far as reaping the rewards of her nefarious deeds. She..."

Kurt's voice trailed off as he stared at Dana. Her eyes were as wide as saucers and her lips formed an astonished "Oh".

"Dana?" he said. "What's wrong?"

"That's it," she whispered.

"Huh?"

"That's it!" she yelled, flinging out her arms.

"Huh?"

Dana rushed across the room to grip Kurt's upper arms, her eyes dancing with excitement.

"What you just said about the left hand and right hand, Kurt. That's the key, the proof of my innocence."

"It's a figure of speech, a cliché, or whatever," he said, frowning. "You've lost me here."

"Listen to me. There was a security system installed in my office complex, with cameras in every room. They didn't work properly, and the bosses were waiting for the company to come back and repair them. Todd said that only one camera actually worked. The one in my office recorded Natalie wearing my clothes, accessing the computer and printing out the material the night it was given to the people who hired her."

"This is good news?"

"Yes! Oh, where has my brain been? Kurt, when Natalie and I were ten years old, she fell out of a tree and broke her right arm very badly. She had to use her left hand for everything for several months. When her arm healed, she refused to switch back to her right hand, saying being left-handed made her different from me, and she liked it."

Kurt nodded. "Go on."

"Natalie doesn't do hardly anything with her right hand after all these years. When I was showing her how to use my computer at the office, she had to reach across the keyboard to turn it on. She also switched the mouse to the left side of the desk. She lifted the papers from the printer with her left hand. Don't you see what I'm getting at?"

Kurt grabbed her shoulders and gave her a fast, hard kiss.

"Dynamite," he said, smiling. "You're sensational. That's proof enough for Bonner to haul Natalie in and grill her. He'll have to follow through on your claim that your twin sister was impersonating you.

He'll have to. Hey, we're rounding third and heading for home.''

''I should have thought of it sooner. I...''

''Shh.'' Kurt wrapped his arms around her and pulled her close. ''All that matters is that we've got the evidence we need to prove your innocence.

''I'll call Pete back right now and fill him in. We both figure that Natalie is going to show up at your apartment soon. Pete will know where she is, so the cops can pick her up. I'll phone Bonner in the morning and explain it all to him from the top.''

''But you'll get in trouble, Kurt, because you've been keeping the fact that I'm here in Montana from Detective Bonner.''

''It'll be fine when the dust settles. Give me ten minutes on the telephone with Pete, then we're going to celebrate.''

''Oh?'' Dana said, smiling. ''Are we going dancing, then having champagne served at our table?''

''No, we're celebrating a little closer to home. Right down that hall, in the bedroom.''

''Do tell.''

''No, ma'am, I prefer show, not tell, remember? Go. I'll be there in ten—make that five—minutes.'' He dropped a quick kiss on her lips.

Dana was smiling as she slipped back onto the bed, not bothering to reach for the sheet. But then her smile faded.

It was almost over, she thought. The nightmare was almost over. They had all the pieces to the puzzle now, and it was just a matter of putting them together to spell out the crystal-clear message that she was innocent of any wrongdoing.

It will all be over soon.

Kurt's words echoed in her mind, and a chill swept throughout her. She should be bouncing on the bed like a cheerleader, rejoicing in the knowledge that the light at the end of the long, dark tunnel was finally glowing brighter and brighter. She *was* relieved, and very grateful, that there was now proof positive that Natalie had committed the crime in question.

But...

It will all be over soon.

She pressed her fingertips to her lips.

Yes, it would. Be over. All and everything she'd shared with Kurt would become memories to keep when she left Whitehorn. And she would take with her, in her aching heart, the unspoken truth that she loved him beyond measure, forever and always.

Kurt appeared in the doorway to the bedroom, and Dana's gloomy thoughts vanished as she lifted her arms to welcome him into her loving embrace.

Chapter Fifteen

The next morning, Kurt headed for the kitchen to make a pot of coffee while Dana finished dressing. They'd showered together, declaring themselves to be good citizens for conserving water.

As the aroma of freshly brewed coffee wafted through the air, Kurt grabbed the bag of cat food and crossed the living room just as Dana came from the hallway.

"Hi," he said, smiling as he passed her. "Coffee is perking. I'll feed the beasts and be right back."

"Yes, sir," Dana said, matching his smile, then turning toward the kitchen.

Kurt opened the inner door, and was about to push the screen when he stopped, every muscle in his body tensing. He stepped out of view, closed the door and dropped the bag, his heart and mind racing.

There were no cats on the front porch waiting for their breakfast.

None.

Okay, he thought, nodding. He wasn't sure he'd believe it if he hadn't seen that empty porch with his own eyes, but...

"Thanks Mom," he said quietly, looking heavenward.

"Kurt," Dana said, from the doorway to the kitchen, "would you like some eggs and—"

"Shh," he said. "Get down."

"What?"

He ran across the room and grabbed Dana's hand. "Bend over. I want you to sit on the floor in the hallway. Move. Now."

"Why? What—?"

"The shooter is out there."

"Oh, God," Dana said, feeling the color drain from her face. "How do you know that? Did you see him?"

"No, but I had a message delivered by a very special lady. I'll explain later. Let's go."

Kurt deposited Dana on the floor in the hall, then dashed into the bedroom for his gun.

"Oh, God," Dana repeated, when Kurt reemerged with the weapon in his hand.

She leaned her back against the wall, pulled up her knees and wrapped shaking arms around them.

"Be careful," she said, her voice hushed. "Please, Kurt, please be careful."

"Guaranteed. Don't move from that spot, no matter what you might hear. Understand?"

Dana nodded, unable to speak further as fear closed her throat.

Crouching, Kurt went from window to window in the living room, peering through the drapes. Staying low, he went into the kitchen, inching up slowly to look out the window over the sink.

"Bingo," he said, under his breath. "You're toast, sleazeball."

The man was making his way forward, moving from behind one tree to the next. He wore black pants and shirt, and was carrying a gun.

Kurt watched him from the edge of the kitchen window long enough to be certain the man was heading for the back door of the house and not intending to veer around to the front.

Satisfied with what he'd observed, Kurt bent over and sprinted to the front door, leaving the house with hardly a sound.

Dana crawled down the hallway on her hands and knees, stopping before entering the living room. She wanted to be closer than she had been, she'd decided, to hopefully hear something that would give her a clue as to what was happening.

Calm down, she told her thundering heart. Kurt knew what he was doing. He was a highly trained professional, who made his living dealing with the bad guys. Men who carried guns. Who had been hired to kill her. Who would think nothing of killing Kurt first, if he got in the way.

Oh, dear heaven, why couldn't Kurt have a safe, pleasant career, like being a mailman or an accountant?

Dana pressed trembling hands to her pale cheeks and waited.

* * *

Kurt made his way along the side of the house to the back and looked quickly around the corner. The man had left the cover of the trees and was running toward the back door, bent over at the waist.

Kurt stepped free of the house, clasped his gun in both hands and planted his feet slightly apart on the grass.

"Police!" he yelled. "Drop it and freeze!"

The man whirled around in the direction of Kurt's voice. In one flash, the man saw the regulation stance, the weapon, and the cold glint in Kurt's eyes. The gun hit the ground with a thud.

"On your belly, spread-eagle," Kurt said, starting forward. "Give me an excuse, scum. That was my lady you were trying to take out." The man flopped down on the ground. "By the way," Kurt said, standing over him, "how's Natalie?"

The next twenty-four hours were hectic.

Kurt called Judd, who arrived in record time and was given a full explanation as to why there was a man handcuffed to the drainage pipe on Kurt's back porch.

Kurt then telephoned Detective Bonner. With Judd's smooth and helpful persuasion, Bonner agreed not to file charges against Kurt for harboring Dana. Arrangements were made to hold the shooter in the Whitehorn jail until he could be transported to Chicago.

Kurt called Pete, who had witnessed Natalie entering Dana's apartment and not leaving. Kurt informed Bonner, and Natalie Bailey was arrested.

Four hours later, Bonner called to tell Kurt that

Natalie had signed a full confession and all charges against Dana Bailey had been dropped.

Kurt had no sooner hung up the receiver than a clerk of the Whitehorn court rang through to announce that the request for a change of venue had been denied and the trial of the man accused of shooting Clem was to begin at nine o'clock the next morning.

"We'll be there," Kurt said, then hung up the receiver. "The trial starts tomorrow," he said to Dana. "It should be short and sweet. So! That ties up all the loose ends, I guess. This calls for a *real* celebration."

No, Dana thought, sinking onto the sofa in Kurt's living room, this called for what she'd been postponing, not indulging in, not allowing herself to have, for many, many weeks now. She was due and overdue. She deserved this, had earned it, it was hers to have.

And with that, Dana Bailey burst into tears.

Kurt jumped to his feet as though he'd just discovered that the chair he was sitting in was on fire. He hurried to sit down next to Dana, sliding one arm across her shoulders and pulling her close. She covered her face with her hands and wept.

"Hey, there," Kurt said, patting her on the back. "The nightmare is over. There's no need to cry now."

"I need to cry now," came the muffled reply, "because I wouldn't let myself cry during the nightmare."

"Oh." Kurt frowned in confusion. "Whatever. You go right ahead and wail your head off, and I'll hold you. Don't rush. I have all the time in the world."

And so, Dana cried.

She cried because of the fear she'd lived in for so many weeks, due to the betrayal of a sister who would never be her friend.

She cried because she'd been shot at and nearly killed.

She cried because in a few short days she would be leaving Whitehorn, Montana, and Kurt Noble, and Kurt was the only man she would ever love.

Dana cried until she was exhausted, her nose was red and her cheeks were blotchy. She accepted the pristine white handkerchief that Kurt offered her and dabbed at her nose.

"Better?" Kurt said gently.

"Guess so," she said, with a funny little hiccup. "I had a lot stored up in my emotional chamber."

"Mmm. Is this emotional chamber at a safe, normal level now? Ready, able, to receive new emotional data?"

Dana dried her tear-streaked cheeks with the handkerchief.

"I suppose so," she said. "That's what good cries are for, to houseclean the emotional chamber."

Kurt framed her face in his hands and tilted her head up so that he could look directly into her shimmering blue eyes.

"Then I have some new emotional data for you," he said quietly, no hint of a smile on his face. He paused, took a deep breath, then let it out slowly. "Dana, I love you."

Dana blinked. "Pardon me?"

"I love you. I am deeply in love with you. I'm humbly asking you to be my wife, my other half, my partner. I'm asking you to live in this house and help me make it a warm, welcoming home. I'm asking you to have my babies and stay by my side until death parts us. Dana Bailey, will you marry me?''

"I...I love you, too, Kurt,'' she said, fresh tears threatening.

Kurt smiled. "Then, hey, that settles it. You'll marry me. Right?''

"No. I can't.''

Kurt dropped his hands from Dana's face and frowned. "Why not? We're in love with each other. We've been through a rough ordeal together, and that love is still strong and steady. We can have it all, Dana, just like we talked about.''

Dana got to her feet, wringing the handkerchief with restless hands. She turned to look at Kurt again.

"Have it all?'' she said. "Aren't you forgetting something?''

"Like what? Give me a clue here.''

"My career, Kurt. I've worked hard and long to become an attorney. It's important to me, part of who I am. What would a corporate attorney do for clients in Whitehorn, Montana?''

Kurt stood, his frown deepening. "You want the life, the world, you had in Chicago more than what we could share together here?''

"That's not fair,'' she said, her voice rising. "You're forcing me to choose one over the other. I'm the only one who would be making any sacrifices.''

"Marrying me would be a sacrifice?'' Kurt said, matching her volume. "Don't knock yourself out.''

"You're not even trying to understand. What about compromise? Why do I have to walk away from a career that means so much to me in order to be your wife?''

"Because your husband would happen to live in Whitehorn, Montana!"

"You're asking too much of me!" Dana yelled.

Kurt stared at her for a long moment. His voice was ringing with pain when he spoke again.

"No, I'm simply asking you to listen to the whispers of your heart," he said. "You've done that, I guess. You've said that you love me, but I'm not enough. What I'm offering you isn't enough. So be it, Ms. Bailey. After you testify at the trial, have a nice trip to Chicago."

"Kurt..."

"I'm going for a walk. Do us both a favor and head for the motel before I get back. I had your car driven out here, and the keys are under the mat on the driver's side."

"Kurt, please..." Dana said, tears spilling onto her cheeks.

"Please what? Move to Chicago with you? Agree to have you live and work in Chicago and come home on the weekends? I can't do either of those, Dana."

He started toward the door, then stopped with one hand splayed on the screen. He looked back at Dana over his shoulder.

"You're not wrong to want a career in Chicago. I'm not wrong to want you here with me in Whitehorn. We're just wrong for each other. I..." He shook his head as emotions choked off his words. "Goodbye, Dana." He left the house.

"Oh, dear heaven, no," Dana said, a sob catching in her throat. "Kurt, no."

We're just wrong for each other.

With the chilling truth of Kurt's words ringing painfully in her ears, Dana stumbled down the hallway to collect her belongings from the bedroom. A short time later, she drove away.

Kurt stood surrounded by vibrant wildflowers on the rise beyond the house and watched Dana leave, not moving until the last particle of dust on the road had settled, erasing all evidence that Dana Bailey had ever been there. Erasing all evidence except Kurt Noble's broken heart and shattered dreams.

Dana turned over the page on the calendar at the top of her desk at the office, then stared at the new number.

It was the middle of June, she thought. She'd been back in Chicago a week, and it seemed like an eternity.

She'd testified at the trial in Whitehorn, then waited to hear the guilty verdict at day's end. An announcement had been made that a party was being held at the Hip Hop Café in Clem's honor and everyone was invited. A cheer had gone up from the jubilant spectators.

Dana had slipped through the crowd and driven away from Whitehorn, Montana, barely able to see the road through her tears. Kurt had been nowhere to be seen after giving his testimony.

Dana sighed and leaned back in her chair.

How long before the pain of missing Kurt began to dim? she wondered.

How long before she could sleep at night, instead of tossing and turning, then dreaming of Kurt when she finally managed to doze?

How long before tears weren't always just a breath away from spilling over?

How long would she feel the chill and emptiness of loneliness?

"Get busy," she said aloud, straightening in her chair.

She pulled a file from the stack at the side of the desk and flipped it open, frowning as she scanned the first page.

And that was another thing, she thought. Her caseload was dry and boring, dull as dishwater. Where had the challenge gone, the enthusiasm for her life's work?

Good grief, she was a wreck. She was a weepy, grumpy nothing-is-right-with-my-life wreck. She had to get her act together right now.

She reached under the desk for the bag she'd brought from home. She removed the small shadow box she'd purchased in Whitehorn and set it next to the calendar. She was unwrapping the tissue from the china kittens when Todd Gunderson came into the office.

"Good morning, Dana," he said, smiling. "How's my favorite attorney?"

She was going to scream, Dana thought. Todd had said that same corny thing every morning since she'd been back. He'd been hovering around, acting as though he had proprietary rights over her because he'd supplied Pete Parker with the information about the video.

Todd was as dull as dishwater, too. There had been a time she thought he was attractive, intelligent and interesting. He was an up-and-coming attorney who would no doubt be made a partner in the firm in the next year or so. But unless he was talking about corporate this or that, he had absolutely nothing to say.

"I'm fine, Todd," Dana said, spreading out the tissue paper.

Todd picked up the shadow box. "What's this?"

"A special little box to hold this figurine of these kittens."

"You're kidding."

"What?"

"Dana, come on. This is a cheap, tacky box made of plywood, and that figurine isn't exactly Dresden china. It looks out of place in this office, like it doesn't belong here. You're trying to make it into something it can't possibly be."

Dana's heart began to beat a wild tempo. She got to her feet slowly and reached over to remove the shadow box from Todd's hand.

"You're right," she said, staring at the little box. She picked up the kittens. "You're absolutely right. When something is out of place, is obviously where it doesn't belong, is attempting to be what it can't possible be, it shouldn't be here."

"Right. So, ditch the junk you're holding there."

"Oh, no, Todd, I'm not talking about the shadow box and my precious kittens. I'm referring to me. I don't belong here anymore."

"Dana, calm down," Todd said. "You've been through a stressful ordeal, you know. Why don't you and I take a little trip, get away for a few days? It will do you a world of good."

"No, Todd, you don't understand. I'm leaving Chicago. I'm going home. I'm going to Whitehorn..."

"Montana," a deep voice said.

Dana looked toward the doorway, and a gasp escaped from her lips.

"Kurt," she said, then remembered to take a much-needed breath of air.

"Dana." He nodded and started forward, no readable expression on his face. He carried a file folder in one hand, and was wearing jeans and a western shirt.

"Do you have an appointment, sir?" Todd said.

"Do you have a life?" Kurt answered.

"Where did you park your horse?" Todd said with disdain, his gaze sweeping over Kurt's attire.

"Stop it, both of you," Dana said. "Todd, please leave my office. I have an appointment with Detective Noble."

"Fine," Todd said, "but what's this nonsense about your not belonging here, about Whitefield—"

Kurt interrupted him. "Whitehorn. Montana. Whitehorn, Montana. Do you know where Montana is, Todd?"

"I'll speak with you later, Dana," Todd said. He left the office, closing the door none too quietly behind him.

"He's a nerd," Kurt said.

"I know," Dana said, unable to tear her gaze from Kurt's face. "What are you doing here?"

"I came to take you home."

Dana's trembling legs refused to hold her for another second, and she sank into her chair. Kurt settled into the chair opposite her desk and propped one ankle on the other knee.

"Take..." Dana cleared her throat and tried again. "Take me home?"

"To Whitehorn," Kurt said, looking directly into her eyes. "To the house you helped make into a home. To the cats on the porch, who will always be welcome now, because they delivered a message to me that I needed to know. To the wildflowers on the hill, and the ones we fly to when we make love.''

"Oh, Kurt," she said, her eyes brimming with tears.

"I came to take you home...with me, as my wife. Did you mean what I heard you say? Were you leaving here, coming to me on your own?"

"Yes. I love you so much. I've missed you beyond measure, Kurt. I don't know what the answer is as far as what I'll do with my training, my love of the law, but..."

"Whoa," he said, holding up one hand. "I've been working on that. I held a meeting at the Hip Hop. I said, 'Friends and neighbors of Whitehorn, I'm in love with Dana Bailey. But, folks,' I said, 'my Dana is an attorney and needs to keep her fingers in that pie to be truly fulfilled. I want to marry that woman and bring her home to Whitehorn. Are you going to help me out here, or not?' That's what I said."

"You did not," Dana said. "You did? At the Hip Hop? In front of everyone?"

"Yep. Hey, I'm a desperate, lonely man, who wants his lady by his side." He shrugged. "The people in Whitehorn thought the whole thing was perfectly reasonable."

"Dear heaven," Dana said, blushing a pretty pink.

"Anyway," Kurt said, flipping open the file, "you've got lots of lawyer-type work waiting for you in Whitehorn. Let's see now. Judd and Tracy, Melissa and Wyatt, and Kate and Ethan, all need wills drawn up. Winona wants a legal document listing everything she has at the Stop 'N' Swap in case she's ever robbed. Travis and Lori feel they should name guardians for their kids. Clint and Dakota..."

"I love you, Kurt Noble," Dana said, smiling as tears spilled onto her cheeks.

She got to her feet and came around the desk. Kurt tossed the file on the desk and rose to meet her with open arms.

The kiss they shared was long and loving, erasing the hurt and loneliness of the past and making a commitment to the future.

"Will you marry me, Dana Bailey?" Kurt said, when he finally raised his head.

"Oh, yes, Kurt Noble," she said, her big blue eyes glistening with tears, "I will."

"Then, Dana?" he said, his voice husky with emotion. "Let's go home.

*   *   *   *   *

MONTANA MAVERICKS: RETURN TO WHITEHORN

continues with

MONTANA MAVERICKS WEDDINGS

**A short story collection by
Diana Palmer, Ann Major
and Susan Mallery**

Available in April

...only from Silouette

Turn the page for
an exciting sneak preview....

Chapter One

Abby Turner of Whitehorn, Montana, was getting married. There never was a more reluctant bride. She stared at the small diamond solitaire on her left hand with sad gray eyes in a pretty face framed by wavy dark hair and wished with all her heart that she'd said *no* instead of *yes* when Troy Jackson had proposed. He was a kind and sweet man, but she knew for certain that within a month of the wedding, she'd be walking all over him. She was a fiery, impulsive woman with an outrageous sense of humor, and she embarrassed him. She'd tried to deny that part of her nature, but it kept slipping out. Inevitably, people noticed.

Whitehorn was a small town where people lived as they had for generations. A ranching community sprawled outside the city limits and Troy, along with his father, ran several hundred head of Hereford cattle on their third-generation ranch. It wasn't as large as Chayce Derringer's spread, but then, Chayce had more money than most local people. He was involved in mining as well as ranching. He'd been Abby's guardian since the death of her father, his foreman. Abby had been ten at the time. Her mother, Sarah Turner, had become handicapped as a result of the same wreck. Chayce had taken mother and daughter right into the big house with his housekeeper, Becky, and assumed total responsibility for them.

Whit Turner, a former rodeo cowboy, had been not only his foreman, but his idol and surrogate father as well. Chayce had loved him. He was fond of Abby, too, and he'd spoiled her rotten. At least, until she was sixteen. That had been when the arguments began, each one hotter than the one before.

Abby had given Chayce fits, not because she was rebellious, but because she was feeling the first stirrings of love for him. He was fifteen years her senior and completely impervious to her, and it hurt. Consequently, Abby's temper grew steadily worse until she was eighteen. She'd pushed him too hard only once, and something had happened that had kept him completely out of her life ever since. It had been almost four years since Abby had seen him at all. He made sure of it.

He'd arranged for her to go away to college as soon as she graduated from high school, just two weeks after their disastrous encounter. It had been traumatic. Her mother had died that same year, and Chayce had been determined that she needed the change of scene—and to get away from him. What had happened, he told her grimly, couldn't be allowed to happen again.

So Abby had gone to college at California State University, taking her degree in business, and Troy Jackson had come to her campus to do some work on his teacher certification. They'd started dating and very soon Troy had proposed. They lived in the same town, he pointed out, and he'd inherit his father's ranch one day. What could be more natural than to marry Abby and have kids to inherit it when he himself passed on?

It had seemed logical. Abby's encounter with Chayce had put a wall between them that hadn't ever come down. He was a fiery and independent man who'd had a devastating love affair when he was little older than Abby was now at twenty-one. He'd never gotten over the loss of his fiancée, and he'd never let another woman close enough to wound him. He'd made it crystal clear that Abby didn't have a chance, despite his headlong ardor that night so long ago.

Abby had just graduated the first week of June, with only Troy and her college roommate, Felicity Evan, to watch her accept her degree. Chayce hadn't come near the campus, although he'd sent a telegram of congratulations.

He wasn't home, now, either, of course. He found reasons to go on long business trips the minute Abby announced any plans to stay at the ranch. She'd written him about her engagement to Troy and asked him to give her away at their August wedding in White-horn. He hadn't replied. She wondered if he would.

She tried not to talk about Chayce, but he was so much a part of her life that it was inevitable that she would. Troy made his distaste for her guardian quite clear, although he promised to tolerate Chayce once he and Abby were married. He only hoped, he told her firmly, that Chayce would be a little more discreet in future about his love affairs. Chayce was handsome and rich and eligible and he was dating a well-known Hollywood starlet. Therefore, it was inevitable that he was photographed with her and the pictures ended up in the tabloids. The publicity nauseated Troy, who was even more conservative than Becky, Chayce's housekeeper.

Because Troy made so many tart comments about Chayce, Abby made sure that she didn't let her own feelings for him show.

She stared at the ring on her finger, wondering what on earth had possessed her to agree. Despite his glacial treatment of her, she loved Chayce. She was never going to be able to give her heart or her body to anyone else. After four long years, that was painfully apparent. But Troy was kind and sweet and after one ardent kiss that Abby hadn't been able to respond to, he'd confined his affection to hand-holding and lazy smiles. Perhaps he hoped that his reticence would succeed where his ardor hadn't.

What he didn't realize was that Abby was incapable of feeling physical desire for him. It was a problem that she hoped they could work out after they were married, but she didn't dwell on it. She couldn't go around forever mooning over a man who didn't want her and who had made it perfectly clear.

"I wouldn't count too much on him agreeing to do it, Abby," Becky said gently.

"But why not?" she replied. "He's looked after me since I was ten."

The gray-haired woman hesitated. She busied herself with the dough. "He has...other interests."

"He could bring Delina with him. She might like to be a bridesmaid. I wouldn't mind." That was a vicious lie, but she told it with a calm expression.

"He wouldn't do that, I'm sure." She added the shortening to the flour. "He's possessive about you. I've wondered ever since you mentioned the engagement if he was going to come back at all while you were still here. He doesn't, usually." She glanced at Abby worriedly. "You must know that he doesn't like Troy."

Abby looked astounded. "No, I didn't know. When has Chayce ever seen Troy in order to dislike him."

"Troy went to talk with him while you were both in school last summer in California," Becky said reluctantly. "To get his blessing to court you. You know how old-fashioned Troy is."

Abby's heart turned over. "Troy never said a word about it!"

"I don't guess so, after what happened." She grimaced. "Chayce told him that you needed to grow up before you thought about getting married. He wasn't pleased at the news. Not at all. I expect when he gets this letter of yours about the wedding, he'll go right through the ceiling, Abby."

Her breath seemed strained. "That's surprising. I thought it would delight him to know that I'd finally be out of his hair."

"He's taken care of you for a long time, Abby," Becky said. "Despite the fact that he's kept his distance all these years, he's kept a careful eye on you. It isn't going to be easy for him to hand you over to another man."

"He doesn't want me around," Abby said with helpless bitterness.

"That isn't true!"

"Yes, it is." Her gray eyes met Becky's blue ones. "He couldn't even be bothered to come to my college graduation. But Troy did. And so did my friend Felicity."

"That isn't why you're marrying him, is it?"

Abby stiffened. "Of course not. I'm marrying him because we have a lot in common and we get along well together."

"Do you love him?"

Abby wouldn't look at her.

*   *   *   *   *   *

THE BABY OF THE MONTH CLUB

RITA Award Winning Author

MARIE FERRARELLA's

miniseries continues with her brand-new Silhouette single title

In The Family Way

Dr. Rafe Saldana was Bedford's most popular pediatrician. And though the handsome doctor had a whole lot of love for his tiny patients, his heart wasn't open for business with women. At least, not until single mother Dana Morrow walked into his life. But Dana was about to become the newest member of the Baby of the Month Club. Was the dashing doctor ready to play daddy to her baby-to-be?

Available June 1998.

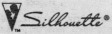

Silhouette®

Find this new title by Marie Ferrarella
at your favorite retail outlet.

Take 4 bestselling love stories FREE

Plus get a FREE surprise gift!

Special Limited-time Offer

Mail to Silhouette Reader Service™

P.O. Box 609
Fort Erie, Ontario
L2A 5X3

YES! Please send me 4 free Silhouette Special Edition® novels and my free surprise gift. Then send me 6 brand-new novels every month, which I will receive months before they appear in bookstores. Bill me at the low price of $3.96 each plus 25¢ delivery and GST*. That's the complete price and a savings of over 10% off the cover prices—quite a bargain! I understand that accepting the books and gift places me under no obligation ever to buy any books. I can always return a shipment and cancel at any time. Even if I never buy another book from Silhouette, the 4 free books and the surprise gift are mine to keep forever.

335 SEN CF2U

Name	(PLEASE PRINT)	
Address		Apt. No.
City	Province	Postal Code

This offer is limited to one order per household and not valid to present Silhouette Special Edition® subscribers. *Terms and prices are subject to change without notice.
Canadian residents will be charged applicable provincial taxes and GST.

CSPE-696   ©1990 Harlequin Enterprises Limited

ALICIA
SCOTT

**Continues the
twelve-book series—
36 Hours—in March 1998
with Book Nine**

PARTNERS IN CRIME

The storm was over, and Detective Jack Stryker finally had a prime suspect in Grand Springs' high-profile murder case. But beautiful Josie Reynolds wasn't about to admit to the crime—nor did Jack want her to. He believed in her innocence, and he teamed up with the alluring suspect to prove it. But was he playing it by the book—or merely blinded by love?

For Jack and Josie and *all* the residents of Grand Springs, Colorado, the storm-induced blackout was just the beginning of 36 Hours that changed *everything!* You won't want to miss a single book.

Available at your favorite retail outlet.

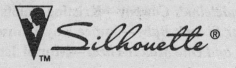

Return to the Towers!

In March
New York Times bestselling author

NORA ROBERTS

brings us to the Calhouns' fabulous
Maine coast mansion and reveals the
tragic secrets hidden there for generations.

For all his degrees, Professor Max Quartermain has a
lot to learn about love—and luscious Lilah Calhoun is
just the woman to teach him. Ex-cop Holt Bradford is
as prickly as a thornbush—until Suzanna Calhoun's
special touch makes love blossom in his heart.
And all of them are caught in the race to solve
the generations-old mystery of a priceless
lost necklace...and a timeless love.

Lilah and Suzanna
THE
Calhoun Women

**A special 2-in-1 edition containing
FOR THE LOVE OF LILAH and
SUZANNA'S SURRENDER**

Available at your favorite retail outlet.

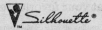

Look us up on-line at: http://www.romance.net   CWVOL2